The S

MW01147416

The Springer Spaniel Mysteries

Written and Illustrated

by

Nancy T. Lucas

Also by Nancy T. Lucas

Courage of a Vampire

The Big Deal, A Charleston Real Estate Caper

ISBN-13: 978-1508647232
ISBN-10: 1508647232

For

my husband John

and our Springer Spaniels: Elwood, Scout and

Benne Wafer

CONTENTS

Part I

May Every Day Be A Dog Party

A MAP OF THE PENINSULA

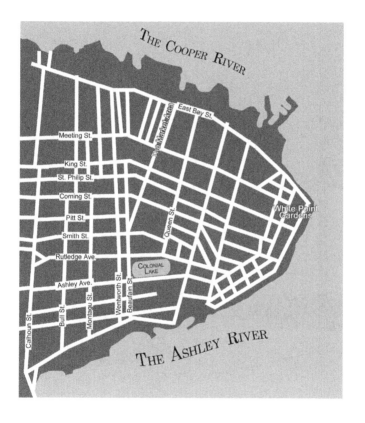

PART I

The Missing Boston Terriers of Smith Street

CHAPTER 1

Scout was very good at being a Springer Spaniel, a bench type of Springer, that is. He sported a solid black blanket on his back and bright white fur around his neck and belly. The feathers on his legs were long and silky. Bench Springers are superior to those field Springers – a mostly white, very little color, long-tailed yappy sort.

And Scout should know since three of the noisy brutes

lived around the corner. He dreaded walking by – they were such a clamorous bunch. They were taunting Scout, whom they knew was a non-practicing gun dog since he was never taken hunting – not a tragedy in his opinion. Guns were loud. But the field Springer group often mocked him from behind their wrought iron gate. Scout wished it were a solid wooden gate so he could more easily ignore them by not seeing them when walking by.

"Ha, ha!" they barked. "Our dad is taking us flats boat fishing today and we're going to catch some ducks too!" The Springers' dad owned a fishing store and was also a guide. The dogs loved riding in his gigantic Ford F350 pickup truck and barking at everyone they met along the way.

Scout pretended not to care that the field Springers had a more exciting life than his. He actually felt a little lonely sometimes, even though he adored his soft Orvis dog nest in the living room with air conditioning and was allergic to bug bites anyway. His dad worked too much to go fishing and his mumma spent too much time staring at computer screens: TV, iPhone and laptop.

Sigh. Surely his fluffy ears were more beautiful and interesting to scratch than whichever celebrity had recently croaked and the hoopla on cnn.com. Really! But Scout did enjoy lolling about on his Charleston piazza, counting his freckles, chasing striped lizards and barking at the postman. He tried to stay busy while he waited for the weekend when he could go to the marina, swim off the boat ramp and fetch a tennis ball.

So while he did feel a little lonely sometimes, Scout also had some dog friends and acquaintances in the neighborhood, besides the boisterous field Springer gang.

There was Tali, a wise old Golden Retriever who lived a few houses down the street. He guarded the sidewalk in front of his house in a regal, lionly way while his mumma fussed over her azaleas. Tali was much appreciated by all

the college students and neighbors. They always stopped
to pat him and speak to him. Scout longed to have access
to a sidewalk like Tali so he could enjoy more attention
from passersby. A high wall and a locked gate separated
Scout from the foot traffic in Harleston Village.

Then there was Pudge. Pudge was a Boykin Spaniel
who had short, dark brown curly hair. He was always on
duty and professional, even after business hours. Pudge
lived next door to Tali and roamed Harleston Village
freely. Scout was even more envious of Pudge's roaming
privileges than Tali's. Scout remembered when Pudge was
little, often lost and far from home. More than once
Scout's mumma had carried Pudge home when they were
on a walk and discovered the puppy beyond Rutledge
Avenue. But Pudge learned his way around the
neighborhood and was now a tremendous source of
information and gossip.

A cat lady lived next door to Pudge, so she certainly did
not count.

Next door to the cat lady lived a Boxer named Zeek.
When his mumma and dad restored their historic house,
like most people, they ran out of money temporarily. They
had no front steps for several months. Zeek sat on his
porch and looked at Scout across the street every day.
However, after the steps were finally installed, Zeek did
not sit on the porch any longer and talk to Scout. He had
to use his backyard for entertainment. Scout missed Zeek.

The only other dogs that lived near Scout were two
Boston Terriers named Ike and Clyde. They had moved to
Charleston from North Carolina a few months ago. Ike
and Clyde were friendly and Scout liked to stop to chat
with them whenever they were outside. They had a nice
wrought iron fence so they could stick their heads out to
say hi. Unlike most dogs, small dogs in particular, they
never yapped rabidly at passersby. In addition, Scout had
heard that some people from Off (people and dogs not

bred and born in Charleston) were ill mannered, but not these two! They were extremely polite. The terriers were outside for several hours every day because their mumma loved to fuss over her manicured garden.

Today Scout was watching a family of lizards patrol the piazza in search of ants and spiders. He had his head on his front paws and his lovely ears displayed evenly on the floor when his mumma came through the gate. She had been out shopping and had a couple of bags that she set down next to him. She rubbed his tummy when he rolled over and positioned his paws in the air. He did not know why he instantly rolled over and waved his legs in the sky every time a human approached. At the last Dog Party, Tali had said it was a spaniel thing. Pudge had been offended because he would not be caught dead in such a vulnerable position.

One of the shopping bags smelled like the clothing store where Minimum Will worked. Minimum Will was Scout's babysitter and sometimes Scout went to work at the store with Will. Scout loved working at the store. He herded people around, making suggestions regarding accessories. He retrieved belts and took them into dressing rooms for customers to try on. Scout was a little miffed he had not been taken to the store on this recent shopping adventure.

Oh well, he thought. Somebody had to be here to scare the mailman. These lizards surely couldn't do the job. They simply scuttled off to a dark corner at the first sign of trouble.

"Hi Scout!" said his mumma. "Guess what? DOGS are coming over this afternoon. I've invited all your friends!" Mumma rubbed his tummy.

Scout was in heaven. It was a beautiful day and they were going to have company! Maybe Ellen would come and bring her three Springers, Daniel the Spaniel, Bella, and Perrin. They did not live in his neighborhood so he did not see them often. He thought he would take a quick nap while Mumma prepared for the guests so he could be fresh and energetic to greet them.

CHAPTER 2

Scout was looking forward to his Dog Party. These little get-togethers were simple: Mumma opened about ten bottles of chilled refreshments for the mummas and put out bowls of fresh water on the porch for the dogs. Dog Parties usually happened in the late afternoon and coincided with something called Happy Hour.

Tali was the first to arrive with his mumma, Mrs. Lackey. He loped into the courtyard, wagging his huge tail, and licked Scout on the head. "Hiya," he said. "Let's go chase squirrels in the back yard!"

They trotted down the brick driveway to the small back yard and began sniffing and peeing. It had rained recently so all the scents had been erased and new ones needed to be placed in strategic areas.

Tali circled the back yard. "Wow, the yard looks great and smells good! SQUIRREL!" He ran after the bushy tailed rodent. The squirrel ran up a tree, stood on the brick wall and sneered at Scout and Tali.

"HA!" he said. "Can't touch this! Can't touch this!" And he sauntered to and fro and patted his bottom. Scout leaped up the wall, almost to the top (he had had a lot of practice) but the wall was nine feet high. Since Scout often chased squirrels in this way, this part of the wall was free of poison oak and fig vine. The rest of the wall in the yard was covered with foliage. "Catch you later, you dumb dogs!" The squirrel scampered over the wall and up the tree in a neighbor's yard.

Scout and Tali knew they would see no more squirrels that afternoon. That rude squirrel would tell all his friends and family a Dog Party was happening and they would steer clear of that back yard for the day.

"Just once I'd like to get one!" exclaimed Scout. "Nobody likes to be mocked."

"We'll get him. Just you wait and see," consoled Tali. "Let's go see what our mummas are doing. Maybe they have food."

By the time they returned to the courtyard, Ellen was entering with her three Springers. Bella, Daniel and Perrin loved visiting Scout because he had a fountain in the courtyard. The first thing all three Springers did was step into the fountain and lie down.

Scout trotted over and reminded them, "No sillies, you drink out of it. It's not for swimming – it's not big enough."

It was true. Each Springer fit neatly on each side of the fountain. There was room for Scout since the fountain had four sides, but he demonstrated drinking from one of the flowing spouts for them. Bella, Daniel and Perrin were unimpressed and unmoved. They preferred to swim.

"OK," said Ellen. "Be good guests and get out of that fountain." She unleashed them and accepted a glass of refreshment from Mumma. Ellen, Mrs. Lackey and Mumma proceeded to the rocking chairs to talk about Ellen's favorite subject: Springer Spaniel Rescue.

Ellen was the unofficial Patron Saint of Springer Spaniels. If there was a Springer in need, a buzzer went off in Ellen's head. She knew exactly where that Springer was and what he or she needed. The SPCA did not have to call Ellen when a homeless Springer was brought in – she simply arrived at the SPCA at the same time as the poor scared Springer. She was amazing and dogs of all breeds were in awe of her. Ellen had saved, cared for, and found homes for hundreds of unwanted Springers. She tirelessly, carefully interviewed hundreds of applicants to match them with the right Springer personality. Her three Springers felt very special because they lived with Ellen.

Bella herself was a rescued Springer. She was found as a puppy in Wilmington, NC on the side of a road. Bella had wavy black hair and loved to chase a ball. She loved to steal cheese too. Once, at a Christmas party, she had snatched a whole block of Vermont sharp cheddar and swallowed it without any mummas seeing her. Because she hadn't left a trace, no one noticed the cheese missing. Scout liked Bella because she had a tremendous amount of energy. He sometimes referred to her as the Junkyard Dog, which Bella thought was pretty funny. She had a great sense of humor and often led the group in mischievous deeds.

Daniel was the opposite of Bella. He was a low energy spaniel and preferred to not retrieve tennis balls. Daniel and Scout resembled each other because they were distant cousins. They were both black and white, had large blockheads and big paws. Daniel sometimes made a good pillow when Scout was tired of chasing Bella.

Perrin was the oldest of all the Springers, eleven years, chubby and not very energetic. Her black and white curly coat was streaked with gray. She tended to put on the pounds easily if not walked every day. Ellen was hers and hers alone since she'd had Ellen the longest. Perrin was not easily separated from her mumma, and now she climbed out of the fountain to follow Ellen to the rocking chairs. Perrin positioned herself right under Ellen's chair so that there would be no rocking. Perrin did not want Ellen to forget about her or miss her.

Daniel stepped out of the fountain and said to Scout, "OK, thanks for swim. That felt good. What should we do now?"

Bella did not need direction. She took off for the back yard to check for squirrels, not knowing that the squirrels had vanished temporarily. The other dogs ran after her.

When they did not find any squirrels, they decided to run laps around the driveway and porch. They ran up the side steps, through the chatting mummas, down the long porch and front steps and back down the driveway. It was a great circuit. Sometimes the mummas had food so they stopped to see if there was extra food for them. After eating some cookies, they continued the race.

On the third lap, Pudge strolled by the front gate. All the dogs barked polite greetings. He did not come in, of course, since he was patrolling. He was looking for the parking attendant who gave tickets to cars parked too long in the same spot.

Pudge knew all the parking attendants. He liked to alert them if a car had been abandoned and required a boot. New attendants did not know quite what to make of Pudge at first. They eventually got used to him and fed him cheese sandwiches, his favorite. Animal Control paid a visit once a year to Pudge's mumma to reprimand her with a fine for letting Pudge roam free, and his mumma usually told them to go away. And they did. After all, Pudge couldn't very well meet his neighborhood responsibilities locked in his own yard now, could he? What were those people thinking?

No more dogs came to the party that day. Scout was sorry Ike, Clyde and Zeek did not attend the party. Zeek's mumma and dad worked long hours, and Ike and Clyde often traveled between Charleston and North Carolina. A few more non-mummas, dogless, came by to help drink the refreshments. Daniel ran into the water bowl on a lap and upset it so Mumma refilled the bowl for the hot tired dogs. By this time, they were all ready to squeeze themselves under chairs, drool and sleep. It had been a great Dog Party, except for the elusive, rude squirrel.

CHAPTER 3

Dad came home and poured himself some refreshments leftover from the Dog Party.

"How was your day?" asked Mumma.

"I would've rather been at the Dog Party with all of you," said Dad. "I think I'll put this in a go-cup and take Scout for a walk. Wanna come with us?"

"Sure," said Mumma. She put on her sandals.

Scout began to hop up and down.

"Stop hopping up and down like a pogo stick, Scout," said Mumma as she opened the front door. Scout ran to the front gate and sat down. This is where Mumma or Dad put on his leash.

Mumma grabbed plastic bags out of a large ceramic frog planter. Mumma did not keep plants alive for very long, so there were always empty planters around the porch and courtyard. This particular frog had held a bushy flower when it was new, so the frog had appeared to have a purple Afro. Then the Afro died, but the frog remained to become a receptacle for plastic grocery bags for Scout's pickups.

Dad set his blue go-cup on the courtyard wall ledge and attached Scout's leash to his red nylon collar. Scout had chewed through all his leashes except this one. He liked to chew when he was nervous. Or happy! Or excited! So Dad had gone to the boating store and bought a length of black and yellow spectra line in which Scout had barely been able to fray.

The three of them set off down the street toward Ike and Clyde's house. When they turned the corner onto Smith Street, Mumma was dismayed. On the telephone pole was a poster:

LOST!
2 Boston Terriers
Ike and Clyde
Last seen: July 7th

REWARD: $200!
Please call 843-555-1234

"Oh no!" exclaimed Mumma.

"How awful," said Dad.

Just then they saw the Boston Terriers' mumma, Karen, coming back with posters and a stapler in her hands. She was very distraught.

"Oh no!" she said. "You have to help us find them!"

"When did you see them last?" asked Mumma.

Scout sat and listened intently.

"Well, they were here in the yard, as usual. I left to go to the grocery store and when I came back the driveway gate was open and they were gone! I think the gate malfunctioned and didn't close after me all the way..."

Oh no, thought Scout. It had taken Pudge a whole year to learn Harleston Village. These two would not last a week! Scout sniffed around the sidewalk and bushes, trying to pick up a scent. That darn rain had washed everything away.

"Well, we'll alert everyone in the neighborhood we know if they're on our email list. That'll be fast," said Mumma.

Karen agreed that was a great idea. She rushed inside to get started on her email alert.

"Hmm," said Dad. "The problem is they're too easy to steal. Anyone could have reached over the fence if the little guys had been sitting on the steps or ledge. They're so friendly. This is terrible. I hope they're all right." He took a swig from the go-cup.

They continued walking, looking carefully under shrubs and in doorways, anywhere a small dog could conceal himself. What if they had become separated?

Just then a scary thought occurred to Scout. What if the two dogs had been stolen for dogfight training? He shuddered. There had been a nasty rumor a few years ago that a Boykin Spaniel two blocks away had been snatched in the middle of the night by dogfight trainers. More awful stories appeared in the local paper about an evil man who ran a huge underground operation for training Pit Bulls to fight to the death. The stolen dogs became the victims and were not given a fair chance to defend themselves, according to Bella.

Bella knew about these victims from listening to Ellen. Ellen knew many horror stories about stolen dogs. Sometimes Bella, Daniel and Perrin could not sleep at night because of the awful things they heard from Ellen or the other Springer Spaniel Rescuers.

Scout shivered. His mumma often let him stay on the piazza while she ran errands on foot. She carefully locked the gate when she left, and she never allowed Scout to stay outside if she even thought there might be a remote chance of it being dark when she returned home. Nine-foot walls, solid wooden gates and a neighbor's stucco house enclosed the property. Scout felt quite safe. Most of the time.

The three of them continued their walk around the block while they pondered over the missing pair. They passed the field Springer gang who bayed and barked. Scout marked his territory in front of them and that sent them into a froth. He marked the newspaper box at the corner, too. Dad laughed at Scout and drank some more of the refreshment. They passed a huge white house that they never saw anyone go in or out of. They passed an enormous freshly restored historic house on the corner of Pitt and Wentworth Streets. It had been for sale forever. They passed a solid gate and some yipping and scrabbling was heard beyond it, the source unseen. They waved to the grocery store owner at the corner of Montagu and Pitt Streets. Karen had already posted a sign in his window next to the weekly specials' poster.

They turned the corner, back to Montagu Street. At Tali's house, he and Mrs. Lackey were outside while she looked at her one azalea bush.

It was July and hot as the dickens, even for Charleston. Azaleas were not due to bloom again until March. But, it appeared to be the only flowering shrub in the yard, so it must be important.

Scout yanked on the leash and pulled Dad forward. Refreshments flew out of the go-cup all over Dad. Dad said a bad word.

"Tali!" said Scout. "Ike and Clyde are missing!"

"I know! Pudge just told me! What should we do?"

"Do you have email?" asked Scout. "Apparently that's what mummas are going to do, but I don't know how to do that."

Mumma and Dad were talking to Mrs. Lackey who was mortified. She worried for poor lost Ike and Clyde.

"No," said Tali. "I don't think my mumma knows how to email. But she belongs to a bunch of clubs. Maybe they can help."

"What if they were taken by a dogfight trainer?"

Tali's eyes grew big. "Oh no. Don't even think that. I hope they're around here somewhere and just lost. Pudge is out looking for them."

"Will Pudge go all the way to Colonial Lake?" Colonial Lake, a concrete tidal pool, was on the farthest end of the neighborhood, many blocks away. The dogs could have fallen in or might be lost in the bushes around the lake.

"No, I don't think so. That's a long way from here," said Tali.

"Hmm," said Scout.

Mrs. Lackey agreed emphatically to keep a lookout for the lost dogs.

Mumma and Dad collected Scout and went on home. Across the street Zeek was nowhere to be seen either. His mumma had taken him out of town for the week to see his Springer Spaniel cousins, so at least Scout knew he was safe.

Now, how could he get out of the house and search the lake?

CHAPTER 4

The next day when Mumma and Dad went off to work together, Scout sneaked out. There was a small hole in the back wall that Scout knew about that led into the next-door neighbor's yard. There was an old piece of plywood leaned up against the gap with a cinder block to hold it in place.

Scout weighed about seventy pounds so it was easy for him to knock over the cinder block and plywood. He just hoped the neighbor's driveway gate was open so he could get to the street. The gate was usually open because the house was bought and sold every two years and renovated nonstop. Scout thought he could get out because today was Tuesday.

Miss Wanda came to clean the house every Tuesday. She was a little lady who wore long skirts and sang Gospel songs to Scout. However, lately she had been listening to her CD player most of the day. Since she kind of lost track of him every now and then, Scout thought he would get her to let him out right away so he could get started.

Sure enough, here came Miss Wanda, singing along as she unlocked the front door. She patted him on the head, went into the kitchen and then to the laundry room. He was briefly distracted by Miss Wanda's lunch. It smelled like fried chicken and he was pretty sure if he stayed close to her, he would receive a tasty treat later. But he tore himself away. Ike and Clyde were more important than fried chicken. Scout planted himself at the back door and she let him out, still humming to herself.

He trotted to the far end of the backyard under the fig tree, looked at the cinder block for a moment, and swung his ample bottom around. Down it went. Then he knocked over the plywood. He carefully looked into the backyard and saw no one. He trotted through the yard to the driveway. Yes, the gate was open. He just hoped it stayed open and he could get back to his yard.

Rush hour was over. People were at work. The only people milling around in the neighborhood were lost tourists who had maps and construction workers who had tools. The two hundred year old homes needed constant work to keep them from completely decaying in the heat and humidity.

Scout had sat under the table of many a discussion about whether the house needed to be painted or should they buy new gutters instead. Scout was glad he wasn't expected to help maintain the house. He did try to keep people organized when they were working on the house. The latest project had been painting the dining room and he missed those people very much. They did not mind if he sat in the middle of the room and watched them work. He did not enjoy the kitchen renovation project as much. There had been too many people to keep track of and not all the workers had been nice to him. But the foreman had been wonderfully kind and Scout had taken good care of him.

Even though he did not see many people around on the street, Scout tried to stay in the shadows for two reasons. It was a hot July day and a black dog in the sun got really hot fast. Also, the only dog that ran free was Pudge. He did not want to be sent to the shelter, even if he knew Ellen would be there. He had serious work to do.

First, he sniffed around Ike and Clyde's house and sidewalk for clues. Nope. However, there was a large, long-haired, calico cat sitting where the terriers usually sat, on the ledge by the front steps.

"Where are Ike and Clyde?" demanded Scout. He was impatient with cats; they always appeared to be so smug it was disgusting.

"Who?" said the cat.

"You know who! Reveal them!"

"Or what? You'll call the cops?"

"Or Animal Control. They'll look for your rabies vaccination tag you're not wearing!"

The cat hissed at Scout and then said, "It's on my other collar."

Scout could relate to this. He himself had a swim collar, red nylon, and a dress collar, leather. Mumma put the tag on his dress collar.

"I'll ask you one more time: where are the two Boston Terriers?"

"Gone." The cat leaped into a bush and hid.

Scout growled but the cat did not reappear.

He continued down Smith Street and took a right on Queen Street. Just a wild guess, he thought. It was easier for him to stay hidden on Queen Street than on Rutledge or Ashley Avenues. He arrived at the lake.

The lake was temporarily deserted. The morning exercisers were gone, and the lunchtime walkers from the university hospital hadn't started yet.

He darted under a large oleander bush and stayed there for the better part of an hour, watching the lake. He wondered if the lost pair could be hidden under another large bush and decided to make his way around and look. The trouble was that there was not much coverage between the large bushes. Still, he would do the best he could.

Scout sneaked from bush to bush on the Rutledge and Broad Street sides. The Ashley Avenue side was devoid of foliage, so he had to go back the way he came. He would be seen if he crossed the baseball field or tennis courts, much as he loved tennis balls and wanted to retrieve some. It was also hot and he wanted to go for a swim. Springers are great swimmers because they have webbing between their toes. But, he restrained himself.

There was tense moment when a walker went by, but

she was absorbed in her iPod and didn't notice Scout huddled in the bush. When he got back around to Queen Street, he decided to be brave and continue down Rutledge, hiding now and then amongst red geraniums in front of some badly peeling houses.

Scout quickly crossed at the stoplight at Beaufain Street and Rutledge Avenue. He darted into the yard of the house on the corner. Open sidewalks made him nervous. He needed to travel from yard to yard. He had been lucky so far and did not want to press his luck. He knew he could find cover in this yard. No one ever cut the grass or trimmed the bushes, and sometimes there was an elderly liver and white Springer sunning himself.

The old Springer was blind, so when he heard and smelled Scout, he called out, "Who's there?"

"Hello! My name is Scout. I'm looking for a pair of lost Boston Terriers. Have they come this way?" asked Scout, drawing closer to the old one so he could be smelled better.

The old Springer said, "Oh, hello there. My name is Chandler. No, I haven't seen any terriers in my yard. I did see a possum yesterday, passing through."

"Oh," said Scout, momentarily distracted. "Where was the possum going?"

"Who can say?" answered Chandler. "He was looking for some Chinese food to eat. I told him he'd have to go all the way to King Street for that. Off he went, very excited." Chandler thought that was amusing.

Scout was curious. He had never met a possum and hoped they were more polite than squirrels.

"Oh, well if you see Ike and Clyde, or if you hear them, please tell them to come home. Everyone's worried," Scout said.

"Oh, where's home? You'd better give me directions to give to them. If they're lost, they don't know how to get home."

"Yes!" said Scout. "Of course!" And he gave Chandler the address and directions to their home on Smith Street.

"Well, it's nice to see you," said Scout.

"Wish I could see you," said Chandler. "Nice to meet you." And he rolled over and fell asleep again.

Scout nudged Chandler to ask him for the nearest escape route in the perimeter. Chandler directed him to a gap in the fence and Scout squeezed through it. Chandler was about thirty pounds smaller than Scout.

Scout found himself in a doctor's office parking lot. He then scooted into a neighbor's driveway that was completely shaded and full of moldy smells after all the rain. This put him across the street from the Wentworth Mansion bed and breakfast. He then crossed Wentworth Street and stayed on the shady side of Smith Street, opposite of the field Springers' house. He just knew they would blow his cover if they saw him.

He was inching along in the shadows when something grabbed his ear. He was pulled into a dark entryway of a house. He was caught!

CHAPTER 5

Scout was relieved. It was only Reggie the Grumpy, a Jack Russell terrier. He pulled Scout in by grabbing his ear with his teeth.

"Psst!" hissed Reggie the Grumpy.

"Ow! What?" said Scout.

"I know what you're up to."

"Up to? I'm just trying to find Clyde and Ike. Have you seen them?" Scout was hopeful. Reggie the Grumpy lived in a condo on the second floor across from the missing dogs' house.

"Yeah," said Reggie the Grumpy. "It was a dark and stormy night…"

"Oh please," said Scout.

"OK," huffed Reggie the Grumpy. His whiskers were quite long and he liked to shake them and huff. "The smaller guy, what's his name…"

"Ike," prompted Scout.

"Yeah. The little guy fell into the storm drain right in front of his house when the city was cleaning it. Nobody was looking. He had gotten out when the lady went away in her car and the gate didn't shut behind her all the way. For a while, he just hung around on the sidewalk sniffing trees. Then the city came and pulled up the metalwork on the drain to clean it out and down he went. The crew had gone to the corner store for hotdogs. Clyde went in after Ike."

"Oh no!" said Scout. "That's terrible. I bet it smells awful down there!" Scout shuddered at the thought of going down the storm drain. He wondered what to do next.

"I dunno," said Reggie the Grumpy. "We're leaving for vacation in an hour or I'd help you out. I think we'll be gone for a while."

"Well, I've got to save them," said Scout.

"You'll never fit down there," said Reggie the Grumpy. "You're too big. I'd fit, but we have reservations at a dog-friendly hotel in the Outer Banks. See ya. Good luck!"

Reggie the Grumpy popped into his house through his dog door. Scout wanted to strangle Reggie the Grumpy for his short attention span, but at least he had received valuable information.

Now, what to do? The dogs had been gone for a whole day and were probably hungry and smelly by now. Scout thought he had better find a way into the sewer to look for them. He recalled an enormous scary hole in the pavement two blocks down in the middle of the street. Dad had mentioned the pothole a few weeks ago and now it was a gigantic sinkhole. Who knew what was down there!

He trotted down the sidewalk quickly. On his way he met Pudge.

"What the heck are you doing out?" asked Pudge. He was standing in front of his house, checking the parking situation. In mid-July there was plenty of parking, so he wasn't having much fun causing people to get tickets and boots. In a few weeks college would start back and he would have a whole new crop of freshmen to torment.

"I'm headed toward the sinkhole. Reggie the Grumpy said he saw Clyde and Ike fall into a storm drain while the city was working on it. I need to look for them!"

"You dumb fluffy housedog. You'll never find your way around down there. And what were they doing out anyway? They're housedogs, like you. Unlike me – I'm worldly." He paused to scratch an ear.

Scout rolled his eyes. "OK then, you'd probably fit down there better then me. Why don't you look? Have you ever been down there?"

"Heck no," said Pudge. "I'm claustrophobic."

"What's that mean?" asked Scout.

"I'm afraid of tight spots." Pudge sat down. "But, I'll tell you a secret. Some of the drains and sewers still empty out into the harbor on the Battery wall."

"Really?" said Scout. All dogs knew where the Battery was, all water dogs, that is. If you didn't have a motorboat or a boat ramp to swim off, it was the next best thing for being on the water. Plus, sometimes the fishermen shared their bait.

"Yes," said Pudge. "My mumma sells houses and she told me all about how the city determines if your toilet empties in the harbor."

"How do they tell?"

"They light a big fire and make green gas go through the pipes and if the green gas ends up in the harbor, you have to buy a different house because the city makes you fix the house so your toilet ends up somewhere else."

"Oh."

"I sure hope there's no green gas when you go look for them."

"What happens if there is?"

"I don't know. Maybe you'll explode?" Pudge hedged hopefully.

"That can't be right or we'd have exploding rats everyday."

"Wouldn't that be cool?"

"Yeah, it would. Maybe it'd work on squirrels."

Pudge shook himself. "Well, let me know how it turns out!" He marched off in the other direction. Scout would get no more help from Pudge.

Scout was peeing on an oleander bush when he saw Reggie the Grumpy with his dad driving by on their way to the Outer Banks. Reggie the Grumpy barked at him.

Scout darted for the hole in the asphalt. He looked down and called the dogs' names. No answer came, so he bravely leaped into the sinkhole.

CHAPTER 6

Scout landed on his paws a few feet down in the dark storm drain. It was not deep and he had plenty of room to run along. The walls and floor were brick and wet.

Since he had no idea what way the terriers would have gone, he decided to head toward Broad Street and the Battery. Coming out through the harbor was probably the only way he could get home; spaniels are naturally attracted to water so he knew he could find his way. But, he reasoned, terriers wouldn't be attracted to water. They would go the opposite way. Now he was confused and did not know what to do. Trying to pick up their scent was fruitless. He reluctantly chose the direction heading away from the water and back to their house.

He inched along in the darkness. Several rats hissed at him. He growled back and they ran away. Back at the storm drain in front of the Boston Terriers' house he found some short hair and decided it belonged to one of the terriers. He rounded a corner and came upon a fat possum.

"Hello," said the possum. "How are you?" He was nibbling on a palmetto bug. Crunch, crunch.

Scout was so stunned that he forgot to growl.

"Palmetto bug?" The possum offered one to Scout.

Scout thought he ought not be rude. "Oh, no thank you," he managed politely, hoping the possum could not see his lack of enthusiasm for palmetto bugs in the dim tunnel.

"Oh well, suit yourself. Who are you?" He started eating again.

"I'm Scout, a Springer Spaniel."

"Hmm," said the possum. "Don't get many Springers down here often. I know one who lives on Beaufain Street but he's brown and white and I can see you're black and white and much bigger --"

Scout interrupted the possum. "How about Boston Terriers?"

"Hmm, let me think. Oh yes, now I remember."

Scout said, "Yes?"

"Oh wait, no, that was boa constrictor. I remember her distinctly now and she didn't look a thing like a Boston Terrier."

"So you've seen them?"

"Oh yes. Ike and Clyde. They were headed toward the crosstown, north, and I said to them, you'll never get out that way. You have to go to the harbor, south, and then be rescued or swim round to the marina or something. Poor things. Anyway, off they went, arguing the whole way. Clyde was blaming Ike for getting them into this mess when they could be napping on their mumma's bed in the air conditioning and anticipating dinner. I actually think it's quite pleasant down here, don't you?"

Scout did not have time for a chatty possum. He wanted to be home in time for dinner so he wouldn't have to eat a palmetto bug. Today was Tuesday and Mumma always went to the butcher shop on Tuesday. That meant he would get something good and tasty in his bowl. Then they would all go into the living room and watch TV. He would gaze at his mumma and try to keep his eyes open which was difficult on a full stomach in a comfy dog nest.

"Hey, where're you going?" asked the possum. "Can I come too?" He ambled after Scout at a surprising rate of speed.

"Sure," said Scout. What's your name?"

"Chisolm," said the possum.

"Do you know your way around the sewer, Chisolm?"

"Pretty well, I should say."

"OK, then, let's head to the Battery."

"Well, there's lots of ways to get to the Battery."

"What's the most obvious way, a way that they would go?"

"I'm not a mind reader," said Chisolm. "Let's just take the main tunnels, the cleaner ones. They might have picked those if they're used to living inside a house."

Scout and the possum walked along together down Montagu Street. Chisolm paused for the odd palmetto bug and still kept up while Scout sniffed and hunted for clues.

The possum suggested they turn right on Coming Street and Scout agreed. It looked drier than the other tunnel that led off under the college.

But, Scout did not have a good feeling about this expedition. He had no idea if he was going the right way. Sometimes, and he knew from experience, he absolutely thought he was doing the right thing one hundred percent the right way, only to find out the next day he was completely foolish and wrong. He hoped this wasn't going to be one of those times.

He wanted to be right the first time. It irritated him to no end how some people could be so right the very first time with no idea of what they were doing. Those people proved that life was not fair to all the people who were never right the first time and had to keep trying over and over to do something right just once.

"Look!" said Chisolm. Scout looked. Up ahead were some tree roots and a large snake was taking a nap amongst them.

"This is Beatrice the Boa I told you about!" exclaimed Chisolm. "Beatrice! It's me, Chisolm! How was the Amazon?"

The snake opened one eye. "Oh, there you are, Chisolm. I haven't made it to the Amazon yet. Can't find the time. So much to do." She closed the eye.

"Really?"

"Really. Now, go away."

"Oh, OK. This is Scout. We're looking for some Boston Terriers. Have you seen them?"

"If I'd seen them, I'd have eaten them. Nothing like a terrier. Yummy!"

Scout decided he should get going. "Nice to see you, Beatrice." He hurried away.

Chisolm followed.

"Good grief!" said Scout. "What if SHE'S eaten them? How do we know she hasn't?"

"Oh, Beatrice would remember. She'd rather fast for a month and catch something unusual than live off ordinary stuff."

"Um, you're the same size as a Boston Terrier," said Scout.

"Am I? Oh no, I guess we'd definitely better get out through the harbor. We can't come back this way! Look! An apple core! My lucky day! I don't often see fruit! I get a lot of chicken wings, though." Chisolm snatched it up, offered it to Scout who declined, and set to snacking away as they wandered to the next intersection at Beaufain Street.

Scout wanted to continue down Coming to Logan and Tradd Streets, but Chisolm was tempted by the market place.

Scout snorted. "That's a gross touristy place that

smells like horse pee." Scout did not want to admit he was terrified of horses.

"No, there are restaurants and children who drop food. It's a cornucopia! A smorgasbord! A veritable buffet!" Chisolm danced in a circle.

"Well, OK, we can detour for a bit. Maybe we can stop in and see Minimum Will at the clothing store?" he suggested hopefully.

Chisolm gave him a cold stare. "A CLOTHING STORE? Do they have food? Why would you go there?"

"They have dog cookies…" Scout caught himself; he needed Chisolm's help so he didn't want to offend the possum. "Or maybe we could stop in and see my friends at Venus Chocolates?"

"WOW! You have friends at Venus Chocolates?" exclaimed the possum. Chisolm was impressed. He had liked Scout to begin with, but this connection was entirely something else, a whole new level of access to the world up top.

"Well, we might have a hard time getting in there by ourselves without Minimum Will." Scout hastily tried to distract the possum with other food ideas and locations. He did not want to make promises he could not deliver. "Let's go try the pub on South Market. Their garbage can is always full."

"OK. I'll keep the Venus Chocolates thing in mind though. That would be SO awesome!" He rubbed his paws together. Fresh chocolate was something to look forward to, and maybe soon!

CHAPTER 7

Chisolm was overly distracted by food: thinking and talking about food and finding and eating food. It was all Scout could do to keep him focused on the urgent matter of finding the lost terriers. Chisolm wanted to detour to every restaurant in the Market to look for food.

At the intersection of Meeting and South Market Streets, Chisolm decided, "Let's go to that French place instead. I've really been craving some canapés," said Chisolm. "Or better yet, moules in a nice curry sauce."

Scout said, trying not to sound too exasperated with the portly possum, "Sure, you go look for moules. Which way is the harbor? Should I just go down Meeting or East Bay Street?" Scout had a rough idea of how the city was laid out. He was seven years old and had spent those years riding around in the back of an SUV with windows on three sides. He just did not want to take a wrong turn if he could avoid it. He hoped he would not offend Chisolm by not going along to look for moules. What were moules anyway?

Chisolm said, "Oh, I forgot. What were we trying to do? Right! Look for lost dogs." He looked around and they set off down Meeting Street. The rats were bigger and meaner closer to the water. They said unkind things to Chisolm.

"Look at the fatty hanging out with a houseplant," said one huge wharf rat almost as big as Scout himself.

Scout's eyes grew big. He did not say anything back.

The possum said bravely, "He's not a houseplant. He's a housedog. There's a difference, you know. Palmetto bug?" Chisolm offered a handful to the rats.

The rats accepted and did not make any more mean comments. They let the possum and dog pass by and go on their way.

Scout hurried along with Chisolm and said, "You know, Chisolm, you're the only nice one I've met down here."

"I try to improve our reputation, but the others don't try at all. You just never know when you'll need somebody's help, or when you'll be able to help somebody. That's my motto – look!"

They stopped. A small dog's collar lay in the tunnel. The nylon had been stretched, like something had pulled it off, and the buckle was still fastened.

"A clue!" said Scout.

"Yes, a clue!" said Chisolm.

"Oh," said Scout. "This means one of them doesn't have an ID anymore. If they go to the shelter, they're doomed."

"What's a shelter?" asked Chisolm.

"Not a good place, most of the time," said Scout. "Maybe Ike and Clyde have computer chips as well…"

"What's a computer chip? Is it crunchy?" asked Chisolm.

"I'm not sure, but it's supposed to be a good thing. Let's go. Maybe they're close by. Should we call out?" Scout sniffed the collar. Yes, it smelled strongly of Ike.

"I don't think we should. Who knows what would answer or find us…"

Scout led the possum down the tunnel. It sloped down and he thought he could smell salt water. "Where do you think we are now?" asked Scout.

"Probably under White Point Gardens. We're close to the end at the harbor, and we haven't found them. Should we go back and try a different route?" asked Chisolm.

Scout wanted to go to the end of the tunnel and look out at the harbor. Maybe they were trapped on a craggy ledge outside, but low enough where passersby could not see them to rescue them.

The end of the tunnel was wide open to the harbor. Scout carefully stuck his head out and looked around for the pair of dogs.

A small voice shouted, "Scout! Look, it's Scout! We're saved!"

The little voice was coming from Ike. He and Clyde

were indeed trapped on a craggy ledge. Ike was collarless.

"What are you doing down there?" asked Scout.

"We were afraid of the green gas that we saw. We didn't want to explode. So we came out here when we saw it coming!" said Clyde.

That Pudge, thought Scout.

Ike added, "Big wharf rats chased us and grabbed my collar. But I squiggled out of it and escaped!"

"How are we all going to get home?" wondered Scout.

Chisolm said, "Scout – you can swim, right? Can't most dogs swim?"

"Yes, I even have webbing between my toes!" said Scout.

Scout did have webbing between his toes. He was a good swimmer. He swam a few times every week at the marina. Most importantly, the marina wasn't too far away and if he swam there, someone would recognize him and call his dad.

Scout started to organize everyone. "OK, Clyde, you hang on to my collar, and Ike you hang on to Clyde. And Chisolm, you - "

"Oh," said Chisolm. "You don't need to rescue me. I'm home. I'll just go on back and look for those moules."

"But the rats, and Beatrice…"

"I'll stay away from the snake. Rats don't bother me too much. You just say hey next time you're walking by the storm drain by your friends' house. See ya!" He waddled off. Water made him extremely nervous and he did not want to see this part of the adventure. He was gone before Scout could thank him.

Scout and the terriers leaped into the water. They clung to each other as Scout paddled his chunky legs and used his tail expertly as a rudder. Luckily, the tide was coming in and helped deliver the dogs to the marina. Still, it was almost a half a mile and Scout was very tired when they landed. Ike and Clyde looked relieved to be on the boat ramp and solid ground. They were not water dogs by nature.

"We're saved!" said Ike. He hopped up and down. "I'm thirsty and hungry!"

"You are in so much trouble," said Clyde. "WE are

ALL in so much trouble." He shook his head. "What are we going to do?"

Scout knew exactly what to do. "You all stay here and I'll get us a ride home."

He saw the Mac the dockmaster across the parking lot and ran over to him. He patted Scout on the head. Scout stayed with him as they walked the grounds. Finally, Mac looked around for Scout's dad. He didn't see his truck and the boat was in its space. Also, it was the middle of a workday. Mac pulled out his cell phone and called Scout's dad.

Dad was frantic, thanked Mac, and sent Mumma immediately to pick up the dogs. When she arrived at the little marina, Scout, Clyde and Ike were enjoying cheese crackers with Mac.

Mumma hugged all the smelly dogs and said, "Well, I guess Scout knows where to takes his friends for fun. You all need a bath!" She called Karen and said she would bring her dogs home; Karen was relieved.

That night Scout ran into Chisolm in his back yard.

"Chisolm!" said Scout.

"Hi – I just wanted to be sure y'all made it home."

"We did. I have a present for you." Scout had carefully hidden a piece of chocolate on the back steps. "It's not Venus Chocolate, but it's chocolate."

"Chocolate! Oh, thank you," said Chisolm. "Would you like some?"

"No thank you," said Scout. "I had a taste earlier."

The two new friends sat in the yard in the moonlight and reminisced about their busy day while Chisolm devoured his chocolate.

Scout asked, "Chisolm, what are moules?"

Just then a wolfish face appeared in the next door neighbor's kitchen window...

Part II

<u>A Ghostly Tail</u>

CHAPTER 1 – A SCARY WOLFHOUND

"Psst!" said the rosemary bush.

Scout, a fluffy black and white Springer Spaniel, sat on his back steps. It was nighttime and he was visiting his back yard before he went to bed. Sitting on the back steps was peaceful; he liked to reflect on the day's events.

The rosemary bush again said, "Psst!" It grew under the kitchen window, a giant, fragrant bush, larger than Scout. Now it shook its sticky green spines briefly.

"Hello," said Scout.

The rosemary bush had never said "Psst!" before, but that didn't mean it didn't have something to say. He thought he should be polite. He wondered what the rosemary bush was going to say.

"Psst! It's me, Chisolm!" A fat possum waddled out from under the bush. Scout could smell him, all fresh and Christmassy. Scout also liked to run through the bush to obtain that festive scent.

"Chisolm!" said Scout. He was pleased to see Chisolm. They'd spent all day yesterday in the storm drains and sewers searching for (and rescuing) Ike and Clyde, the lost Boston Terriers of Smith Street.

"Hello – I just wanted to be sure y'all made it home."

"We did! Ike and Clyde were so pleased to get home and be with their people. The storm drains and sewers were kind of scary."

"Well, I love it down there. I find it quite pleasant." Chisolm wasn't bothered, just surprised others might find the tunnels scary.

"Oh – and I have a present for you." Scout had hidden a piece of chocolate on the back steps.

"Chocolate! Oh, thank you," said Chisolm. "Would you like some?"

"No thank you," said Scout. "I had a taste earlier."

The two friends sat in the yard in the moonlight. They reminisced about their busy day while Chisolm devoured his chocolate.

Scout asked, "Chisolm, what are moules?"

Chisolm had mentioned wanting to have some moules earlier that day when they were in the Market area.

Suddenly, a dog's face appeared in the next door neighbor's kitchen window... a large wolf-like face. His eyes glowed a fierce red.

"What's that dog over there?" ask Chisolm.

"What dog?" asked Scout.

"There, in that carriage house window," Chisolm

pointed at the house that bordered the west side of the yard.

"I don't know," said Scout. "Our neighbors don't have a dog. Maybe he's visiting?"

Just then, the wolfish face disappeared. Scout thought the face had a transparent quality to it. The thought gave him an eerie feeling.

Chisolm, as usual, was rambling on about food. "Moules is a French word for mussels, a shellfish, much like a clam or an oyster. You boil them up and add some curry and garlic broth. Then, when you eat the moules, you use a crunchy French bread to soak up the sauce. I find it quite filling. I often can't eat French onion soup and moules in one sitting."

But Scout was thinking about the unfriendly looking face in the window next door.

Later that night, as he was sleeping in the second floor hall, he heard barking coming from next door. He looked out the hall's glass French doors. They faced a window of the other house.

The wolf face appeared and made mean faces at him. He could hear the beast barking: "You there! You're nothing but a dumb fluffy housedog! Fluffy is really stupid! You better watch out!"

Then it disappeared.

CHAPTER 2 – AT THE STORE

It was another perfect day in Charleston to be a Springer Spaniel on the piazza. Scout lay on his back with his paws in the air, the light breeze ruffling his fur. His people were at work and he missed them. Some bright green lizards strolled by and Scout ignored them. He was too sleepy to chase them.

Miss Wanda, a nice lady who wore long skirts and sang songs to Scout, came to clean house on Tuesdays. In the morning, she put him out on the piazza by tossing a peanut buttered cookie. Scout scampered after the cookie, gobbled it down and licked all the peanut butter off his paws. Scout was already thinking about lunch. Miss Wanda's lunch smelled like roast beef today and sometimes she shared it with him.

Just then, Minimum Will came bounding through the front gate, iPod buds in both ears. Scout's mumma called Will a minimalist, or Minimum Will for short. Scout thought that was because Will's apartment didn't have any furniture in it. Or food. He wondered what Will ate when he wasn't at Scout's house eating peanut butter or cheese crackers.

"Hey Scouty!" he said. "It's your lucky day. I'm taking you to work the rest of the afternoon at the store." Will rubbed Scout's silky white tummy.

Scout was very pleased. Will often housesat for Scout when his people were going to be home late or out of town overnight. Will watched a lot of cable TV, did his laundry and Scout did not have to be alone. Scout wasn't fond of spending hours alone in the house. He was an only dog and sometimes lonely.

Miss Wanda appeared at the kitchen porch door and said, "Hey, Will! What are you doing here?"

"Hi, Miss Wanda. I'm going to take Scout with me to

work. My manager asked for him. He entertains people while they wait in line to pay."

Scout leaped up, raced to the front gate and hopped up and down. Then he sat as Will fastened the black and yellow leash to Scout's red nylon collar.

"Well, OK then. I'll miss you, Scout! Bye, Scout!" Miss Wanda waved her feather duster.

As soon as they stepped out the front gate, Scout inspected the trees and wall for new smells. He peed on a tree to make sure all the other dogs in the neighborhood remembered that this was his house and his trees.

Scout pulled on the leash as hard as he could while Will ran and tried to keep up. Scout loved working at the clothing store. He helped women choose accessories such as belts or scarves and he was praised and patted. He had to be extremely careful not to drool on anything. One time he had drooled on someone's silk skirt. The head office said he wouldn't be able to work if he drooled on anyone or anything again. So Scout made sure to shake the drool off his mouth before going into the store. His lips made a magnificent flapping sound as he shook his big blocky head; drool flew off him in every direction.

Scout adored King Street the way Chisolm loved the Market area's vast array of food. People were nice to him and patted him as he waited on street corners to cross with Will. They asked his name, how old he was, what kind of dog he was. It was a common question because he was a large Springer Spaniel. He just happened to weigh about the same as a small Labrador, sixty-five pounds. His head was large and squarish; his white paws with black freckles were extra chunky. He was a very sturdy Springer Spaniel.

Today King Street was bustling. The store contained a steady stream of shoppers: people on vacation, students and locals. The other sales people greeted Scout enthusiastically. Margie, the manager, gave Scout a hug and then he headed toward the checkout counter. That's where the cookies lived. He stopped to be patted by every single person in line, enjoying the oohs and aahs.

Then he went behind the counter where Carla, another sales rep, gave him several bone-shaped dog cookies. He thought they were slightly flavored toward the bacon end of the dog cookie spectrum.

After he ate the cookies, he rolled on his back and waved his paws in the air. The hardwood floor was nice and cool.

Carla said, "Oh, Scout! You are so silly! And soft! And sweet!" She rubbed his fluffy tummy and gave him another cookie. People in the line craned their necks to see Scout's paw-waving performance behind the counter.

One of the women was Scout's next door neighbor, Betsy. She and her husband, Bob, had moved in a few years ago. Scout knew they had no children or pets, which is why he was curious about the wolfish dog in the window he had seen for several nights now.

So his ears twitched when he heard Betsy say to Will, "Will, we're going to Alaska for two weeks. We know you often housesit for Scout. Would you want to housesit for us?"

Will said, "Well, sure. When are you going?"

"We're leaving on Saturday."

"OK," said Will. "You don't have any ghosts do you? Because your house is twice as big as Scout's and he has at least two ghosts." He laughed a little nervously, really hoping there would be no ghosts.

"Well, Bob says he's heard some things, but I haven't. I guess I'm just not open to the experience like he is. Maybe Scout can keep you company. He is an excellent dog."

Scout had come out from behind the counter now and Betsy rubbed his ears. He liked these neighbors very much.

"That sounds awesome," said Will.

"I'll let Bob know. See you!" She gathered her shopping bags and left.

"Just as long as there aren't any ghosts," Will said to Carla.

Carla said, "Who's got ghosts?" She rang up the next lady's pants and socks.

Will started folding wool cardigans on the table nearest the register. "You wouldn't believe it. Scout's house has at least two. Two that I know of."

"Who were they? Do the owners know? I'd have an emergency séance and say 'Get out now. This is my house!'" She finished placing the customer's clothes in a silver-colored store bag.

The customer added as she swiped her credit card, "Yes, I have a ghost or two myself out on Sullivan's Island. I think everybody should have at least one. That way you know you're living in an old house."

Will said, "I can do without any ghosts. These are two girls about eight and ten years of age, dressed in Victorian clothing. They wander around in the hall outside the guest room."

"Are they friendly?" asked Carla.

Now all the customers at the register counter were listening. Scout sat up and listened too.

"I guess so. Scout doesn't bark at them, so they must be OK. It's just really disturbing."

It was true. Scout had seen the ghosts and he did not bark at them. They appeared to be able to see him and tried to pet him. He did not care for the way their ghostly hands when right through him, harmless enough, but he knew they could not help it.

Will continued to worry about ghosts, greet customers and fold clothes. Most of the clients knew Will and asked for his help choosing clothes, colors and sizes. Scout tried to help but around four in the afternoon the store became more crowded so he went behind the counter and took a nap.

After work Will walked Scout home. The day was hot and muggy. Scout tried to grab a bagel from an alley but Will steered him away from the discarded bread. Scout thought it wonderful that Charleston's streets were full of food just thrown on the ground everywhere. Barbequed chicken wings, bagels, pizza, muffins, burritos. Every walk was a picnic of culinary surprise!

They were watching TV when Scout's mumma came home and said to Will, "We're going on vacation on Thursday after work. Can you housesit for us and Scout?"

Scout's ears perked up. He was sad when his people went away, but always glad for Will to babysit him.

Will turned down the volume on the TV.

"Oh no!" said Will. "I'm supposed to housesit for Betsy and Bob next for two weeks. How long will you be gone?"

"Only a weekend."

Will thought for a minute. "I can go back and forth between houses. Maybe we could sleep over there. Betsy says she doesn't think they have ghosts."

"I've never heard of any ghosts in that house," said Mumma. They had lived on Montagu Street for a long time and knew most of the neighbors' houses.

"I hope so," said Will.

Mumma went downstairs to feed Scout and Will went back to watching TV. As Scout trotted behind his mumma, Scout wondered about the ferocious Wolfhound next door. Maybe HE was a ghost? He quickly forgot to worry because mumma added some tasty beef brisket to his dry dog food.

CHAPTER 3 – A CHAT WITH PUDGE

Scout was still thinking about the scary Wolfhound's face he'd seen in the windows next door. He dreaded spending the night over there and worried about what might happen. Could ghosts hurt him or Will?

He lay on his piazza while he watched dark brown palmetto bugs crawl around.

Today was pleasantly humid and warm. It would have been suffocating in the sun, but the piazza provided shade and trees shaded the courtyard. Scout dozed, listening to the fountain's soothing trickle of water. He pondered getting into the fountain if the afternoon warmed up more. He knew that was a silly idea. The fountain was only just big enough to step in and lie down, but it would be a nice break from the heat.

Suddenly, there was a "Psst!" from beneath the

boxwood hedge in the courtyard.

Scout walked over to the front steps and looked down at the hedge.

It was Chisolm. "Hi there! What's up?" The chubby gray possum was snacking on a palmetto bug. Crunch, crunch.

"Nothing much," said Scout. "My people are away so Minimum Will is housesitting. On Saturday we're housesitting next door too."

"Oh," said Chisolm. "That's great! I'll stop by and check on you over there." Chisolm waved a palmetto bug toward the house. "I want to try their back yard and see if they have any good snacks!"

"What kind of snacks?" asked Scout.

"Well, the usual, of course. Palmetto bugs, maybe check out the trash can."

"Oh," said Scout. "Please do! I don't want to be over there alone. I think there's a scary big dog in the house. He barks at me through the windows and says unkind things."

Chisolm stopped snacking and said, "What kinds of unkind things? Why would he do that?"

"I don't know," said Scout. "He says I'm a dumb fluffy housedog and that being fluffy is stupid!"

"Well," said Chisolm. "He must be utterly clueless. I enjoy being fluffy. It's a marvelous way to be. So don't be afraid of him and I will stop by to make sure you're OK!"

"Thanks, Chisolm," said Scout.

"Oh, it's not a problem. See you later!"

The portly possum waddled off, climbed up a tree and disappeared.

Scout heard the approach of a carriage tour so he ran to the gate and then back to the steps, barking the all the while.

The carriage tour group, pulled by a pair of brown mules wearing heavy harnesses, rolled up and stopped.

The pale tourists looked sweaty. They were packed into the canopied wooden cart. The word "carriage" did not really apply in this case.

Scout's house wasn't officially on the tour but he loved to bark at mules. The guide had stopped the cart to expand on the house next to Scout's, the one that now housed an obnoxious wolf-faced dog.

There was no sign of the rude beast.

A few of the tourists noticed Scout barking and strained to see his house. The house was set off the street behind a high stucco wall with several trees in the courtyard. It was difficult to see so they lost interest and stared at the official house on the tour. The front door held a stained glass window and the rest of the woodwork was immaculately varnished.

Meanwhile, the guide continued, "And if a gentleman saw a lady's ankle, he had to marry her on the spot!"

The mules looked very bored. They had heard the guide's tour a thousand times and could have given it themselves if anyone would let them. Scout also had heard this part of the tour too many times to count, sometimes three or four times in a single day. The guide finished his tribute and the cart rolled away.

Pudge, a Boykin Spaniel, strolled by the gate. He, too, looked bored. The parking attendants did not ticket cars much during the summer, so he was off duty and looking for chicken wings on the ground.

Scout barked from under the gate, "Hey Pudge! What's up with the wolfhound next door?"

Pudge lived across the street and roamed the neighborhood off-leash all the time. He was a fantastic source of information and gossip.

"What?" said Pudge. "There's no dog in there. You've lost your marbles, Scout." He sniffed the trunk of a crape myrtle on the sidewalk. Then he peed on it.

"No. It's true. It's a big wiry Wolfhound and he says unkind things to me."

"Hmm," said Pudge. "What sort of things?"

"Things like I'm funny-looking and that being fluffy is stupid. I'm very fluffy. Fluffy isn't stupid!" Scout was proud of his black fluffy ears and sleek coat.

Pudge was unimpressed. Being a Boykin, he knew a thing or two about fluffiness and curls himself. Then he said ominously: "I wonder if it could be old Hamish come back to haunt the place."

"Hamish!" exclaimed Scout. "I remember him. He's been gone for years. I think he went to dog heaven before his people moved out... Boy was he a pain in the butt. He bit me on my ear twice! Then he put my head in his mouth!"

How could Scout have forgotten Hamish? Hamish had been truly terrifying. He was three times bigger than Scout, charcoal gray and wire-haired. He had indeed put Scout's whole head in his mouth. Scout, unharmed and but scared, had been gooey with drool.

After that incident, Scout had frantically run the other way whenever he saw him coming. Scout and his mumma tried to elude Hamish by rounding any corner to avoid being seen. They even huddled in bushes or crouched behind garbage cans. Hamish and his family had lived in the house for only a short while, but he had cast a legendary pall on Montagu Street.

"I don't think he went to dog heaven," said Pudge. "Somewhere, but not there... ,"

Pudge paused and then added, "He bit me once in my own yard. Then he bit my mumma! My mumma was very angry with his mumma."

Now Scout was worried. "Pudge, Minimum Will and I are supposed to spend the night in Hamish's old house on Saturday! What will we do if we see Hamish coming at us?"

"I just wouldn't go if I were you," said Pudge. Then he strolled off. Pudge always gave sound advice.

CHAPTER 4 – A SLOW DAY

Thursday morning was a very sad day. Scout watched as Mumma and Dad zipped up their matching gray suitcases and headed out the front door. He knew they were going away.

Before they left, they patted him and told him how much they loved him. Dad gave him a big cookie covered in peanut butter that would stick to Scout's lips for hours. They rubbed his tummy and Mumma even played pat-a-cake with him. Scout lay on his back, paws in the air. Mumma sang the song and patted his chunky paws with her hands. Mumma did not really know the words so she made them up, the last line being, "And baby and me, we want a slice!"

And then a round of "Aws," from both of them.

So off they went, lattes in one hand, suitcase handles in the other.

Scout went to sleep in the front hall on the soft padded rug.

He woke up and moved to his green dog nest next to the fireplace in the living room. He curled into a ball, one ear hanging over the edge of the cushion, and napped.

He woke up later and went into the kitchen to drink some water. He had matching ceramic bowls elevated on a metal stand. The bowls were painted festively with cartoon dogs in party hats and the words "dog party". Underneath the bowls' stand was a yellow and blue folded beach towel to catch any water or food that might fall out of Scout's mouth. That happened a lot.

He wandered into the dining room where he found an old rawhide chew-bone under the table. He chewed on it for a while. After he finished it off, he spotted on old friend, a woolly gray cloth sheep that bahhh-ed when he squeezed it. The sheep was a Christmas gift; Santa had left

it in Scout's bone-shaped red stocking. So he grabbed it
now with his mouth and ran up and down the stairs with
the sheep bahhh-ing all the time. He stopped after a while
because it wasn't any fun unless Mumma was there,
watching and saying, "Aw, how cute!" The house was
terribly silent and his toenails clicked loudly on the
hardwood floors. The tag on his collar jingled too
brightly.

It was such a slow day that Scout fell asleep again in the
front hall and did not wake until Will arrived later that
afternoon.
"Hi Scout! Ready for a walk? I need to go to my place
and get my laundry,"

Scout hopped up and down. He butted the storm door open with his nose. It did not latch since Dad had installed extra door insulation, which defeated the purpose of the extra insulation. So if the front door was open, he could easily open the storm door. He ran to the front gate and sat down. Will attached his leash and they headed to Will's apartment on Meeting Street.

Minimum Will's apartment was located close to his job. Scout only saw a bed in the apartment and lots of space for Scout to run around. In addition, as far as Scout knew, Will did not own a car. He'd never ridden in a car with Will, so he maybe he didn't have one.

Now Will, wearing his backpack, grabbed a full laundry bag and slung it over his shoulder. They were ready to go back to Scout's house.

Outside on Meeting Street, the firemen next door to Will's apartment building all came out to say hi to Scout. Scout thought it sad they had no dog, only a concrete statue of a Dalmatian curled up asleep in front of the firehouse. Scout wondered if he could get a job with the firemen when he wasn't working with Will. He thought it would be exciting to ride along in the fire trucks and stick his head out the window. He loved to howl when the big red engines roared by the house. He had the sirens' pitch down perfectly!

Scout and Will continued their walk. Since Will was listening to his headphones and speaking to people he knew on the street, Scout was free to gobble up any food lying on the sidewalk. He snagged a barbequed chicken wing in front of a shop on King Street and a piece of pepperoni pizza on Wentworth Street. Chisolm would approve! Scout wondered what Chisolm was doing now. Probably sleeping or eating. Or searching for food.

"Scout! Drop that!" commanded Will, suddenly noticing Scout with the pizza. Scout gulped it down hurriedly. He knew Will wouldn't try to take it out of his mouth. Walking with Will was such a little vacation all in itself.

Scout did not find any more food. They stopped at the corner grocery on Montagu Street so Will could buy a newspaper and some chips. Scout waited outside excitedly, hitched to a "No Parking" sign. He knew this store was where all kinds of cookies, chips and cheese crackers came from.

A sign on the door sadly stated "No Dogs Allowed". Scout suspected that sign was placed in the window after a woman and two annoying yip-yaps were always in there, screeching away, scaring the customers. Those dogs had moved away, or at least Scout had not seen them in a while. However, the sign remained, so Scout sat outside and waited.

Back at Scout's house, Will fed Scout and freshened his water bowl. Then Will started a load of laundry.

That night as Will slept in the guest room, Scout lay in the moonlight in the hall. He could see the neighbor's house out of his French doors. Suddenly Scout thought he saw something move. Yes, there it was again! A large wiry, hairy tail was swishing the curtains back and forth at a window. Scout sat up and moved to the doors, pressing his nose against the glass. Then the scary wolf face appeared, snarling at his.

It barked at Scout loudly. Scout could see the old glass in the window shaking against the vibration of the sound. How could a ghost make such a sound? Surely Scout was mistaken. He listened intently.

The wolf was barking: "You there – you dumb fluffy housedog! You better watch out! I'm going to get you! I see you looking at me and you'll never be as cool as me! Being fluffy is a stupid thing! HAHAHAHA!" And then the face vanished.

Scout was bothered by all this and did not sleep well the rest of the night. At least his own ghosts did not show up to further scare him.

CHAPTER 5 – THE POLTERGEIST

Scout and Will went to Betsy and Bob's to housesit. They checked out the kitchen first and Will was happy to find some cheese crackers to share with Scout, which pleased Scout.

They went to the TV room on the second floor and Will found a marathon of reality shows on the Reality channel. He plopped down on a big green leather sofa in front of the wide screen TV. He'd also rented some scary movies on DVD to watch later.

Scout fell asleep immediately. Plotless shows bored him and scary movies scared him. He preferred romantic thrillers, like the movie "To Catch a Thief".

Scout woke up under the coffee table. On the TV some women were climbing a volcano. The volume was turned low. He could hear heavy breathing.

He edged out from under the small metal table. Will was asleep on the sofa. Scout thought that the heavy breathing wasn't coming from Will because it seemed loud and deliberate.

"Haaah, haah," wheezed the breather.

A shadow rose up from behind the sofa. "What are you doing in my house!" demanded the Wolfhound.

Up close, Scout could indeed see it was Hamish. A ghostly Hamish. He was semi-transparent. Scout couldn't decide if he was scarier as a solid or semi-solid two hundred pound dog.

"We're house-sitting," explained Scout. "Would you like a cheese cracker?" Scout looked around for the box and saw it had been ripped to shreds, all the crackers eaten. Crumbs littered the floor.

"Oh no!" said Scout. "I didn't do that!"

"Ha ha!" sneered the Wolfhound. "But HE will think you did and you'll be punished! I ate all the crackers and tore up the box. Just to make a mess that you'll be blamed for!"

"That isn't very nice!" said Scout. He was worried Hamish might bite him on the ear again.

"I'm going to bite you on the ear again," growled Hamish and he lunged at Scout.

Scout was quicker; he scrabbled to turn around and run. Down the stairs he flew to a door he knew opened on to the piazza. Hamish galloped behind him. Scout ran outside, down the steps and into the back yard.

It was cloudy night so the moonlight was dim. He wondered what to do. Maybe he should try to get home through the gap in the wall under the fig tree. Hamish was bounding after him.

Then Hamish stopped. He stared and started quivering. "No!" he cried out. "No! It's a... it's a... POSSUM! Run! Run!"

Chisolm, suspended by his tail from a scuppernong tree, was having a midnight snack of the yellow grape-size fruit.

"Hello," said the possum. "Scuppernong?" He held out a piece of the fruit to Hamish and Scout.

Hamish fell to the ground, his nose on his big hairy paws, whimpering.

"Oh yes," said Chisolm. "I forgot Wolfhounds are afraid of possums! Is there something wrong, Scout?"

"Well, he was mean to me and ate all the crackers while Will was asleep. Then he tore up the box and threw crumbs all over the room. Will might blame me!"

"Goodness!" said Chisolm. "Who'd've thought. A Wolfhound poltergeist. What an awful combination!" said Chisolm.

"What's a poltergeist?"

"A poltergeist. A ghost who can throw things around and make a mess, sometimes loudly."

"Oh that sounds scary!" Scout looked at Hamish. "You there! Stop being mean, loud and messy!"

Hamish rolled over and waved his paws in the air. He

was hypnotized by the possum.

Chisolm slowly pulled himself upright onto a tree limb. "I like hanging upside down every so often. It's a nice change of scenery. These scuppernongs are very refreshing, a nice change from palmetto bugs." He munched on the fruit some more and looked at Hamish thoughtfully. The hound was motionless.

"Well, this is quite a turn of events," said a relieved Scout. "How did you find out Wolfhounds are afraid of possums?"

"Oh, I think my mumma mentioned it once when I was quite small. What should we do with him now?" They stared at the gigantic dazed hound.

"Hmm," continued Chisolm. "Maybe we should command him to go to the Market, scare everyone out of a restaurant and then we can eat all the food?"

"That's silly," said Scout. "Maybe you could command him to go away. Go find his people that moved and go live with them."

Suddenly they heard a small voice say, "Look! Clyde, it's Scout and Chisolm and a scary ghost dog!"

Ike and Clyde, the Boston Terriers, had popped out of their dog door next door. They were peering at them through the fig vine-covered fence that separated the back yards. Their eyes bulged in surprise.

"Hello," said Chisolm. "I'm Chisolm. Scuppernong?" And he held out a piece of fruit.

Clyde shook his head and then said, "Hello again, Chisolm. Thank you so much for helping Scout rescue us from the harbor! Our mumma was sure glad to have us back!"

"Yes," squeaked Ike. "We much prefer being at home than in the storm drains. We were lost!"

"No problem," said Chisolm. "You're very welcome. I know my way around the storm drain and sewers quite well if you ever decide you want an official tour."

"What are you going to do with that ghost dog?" asked Ike.

Just then Pudge arrived.

"Wow, look at that!" he exclaimed. His eyes goggled at the large Wolfhound ghost. "I forgot to mention Wolfhounds are hypnotized by possums."

"Yes, that information might have been helpful yesterday," growled Scout. "He scared me tonight in the TV room. Now he has me framed for making a mess of cheese crackers when Will wakes up. I'm doomed."

"There's no telling what else he's messed up in the house," said Chisolm.

"Yes," said Pudge. "I'll just bet there are dog-shaped dents on all the beds, and slobber spots on all the pillows."

"And hair everywhere!" added Ike, trying to be helpful.

Pudge scoffed. "Ghost dogs don't leave hair everywhere, you silly terrier."

Ike sulked, rebuffed.

"Well, then," said Clyde. "I think we silly terriers should go on back to our indoor dog nests." He led Ike away and back through their dog door on the porch.

Scout was depressed now. How could he show Will he had not been sleeping on all the beds and littering the rooms with cheese cracker crumbs?

The three friends sat on the thick grass for a while and thought.

CHAPTER 6 – THE IDEA

Suddenly, Chisolm had an idea, but he would need a few minutes to carry out his plan.

"Quickly," said Chisolm. "Help me gather more palmetto bugs."

"Chisolm," said Scout. "This is no time to think about food!"

"No, no," said Chisolm. "I can intimidate him with palmetto bugs. All dogs cringe when they think about palmetto bugs."

"That's true," said Pudge. "I think they're slimy. My mumma has the house and yard sprayed often but we still can't keep them out. I'm terrified of palmetto bugs. You guys are on your own." He marched off down the driveway.

They searched the bushes and the bugs scuttled around. Chisolm nimbly scooped up a dozen of the big brown insects.

He waddled over to Hamish and said, "Hamish! Wake up!"

Hamish opened an eye and cringed at the sight of the gray rodent.

"What?" he growled.

"If you don't clean up the mess you made, I'll put these palmetto bugs in your house. Once they're in, you'll never be free of them. So what do you say?" Chisolm waved a bug in Hamish's face.

"No, please!" He squirmed.

"You have to smooth out all the beds, turn over all the pillows and clean up the cheese cracker crumbs before Will gets up. And the shredded box."

"And anything else you did to make me look bad!" said Scout.

Hamish said, "I'll need help to get it all done in time before morning! I've done so many bad things." He squirmed some more.

Chisolm rolled his eyes and looked at Scout.

"What do you think?" said Chisolm.

"I have no choice. I'll start on the third floor and look for things amiss and out of place," said Scout.

Chisolm happily ventured, "I'd better start in the kitchen! I'll take Hamish with me to make sure he points out where all he's been bad to be positive we get everything clean and straight. Maybe there will be more yummy crumbs in there!" He rubbed his paws together in anticipation of tasty treats.

Hamish reluctantly arose and followed Chisolm into the house. Scout headed up the carpeted stairs to the third floor.

He was mortified by what he saw in the first bedroom. Indeed, there was a large dog-shaped dent in the bed and the silk pillows had been tossed on the floor. First he straightened the creamy white blanket by pulling the edges up with his teeth. Then he shook out the beige pillows and placed them back on the bed.

He wondered what was keeping Hamish and Chisolm. There were five bedrooms and he had to straighten every bed and replace all the pillows, making certain the drool spots were not visible.

When he finished the last bedroom, still wondering where Chisolm and Hamish were, he returned to the TV room. Will was still sleeping soundly on the sofa. Chisolm was eating the last of the cheese cracker crumbs. Hamish was sweeping up bits of cardboard box into a knocked over garbage can with his long wiry tail. Chisolm righted the waste can when Hamish finished sweeping.

"All right," sneered Hamish. "Are you guys satisfied now?"

Chisolm waved a palmetto bug at Hamish, who cringed. "No more of that, you bad dog!" said Chisolm.

"What's wrong with you?" Scout said to Hamish. "I offered you crackers. I was happy to share. You didn't need to be bad!"

Hamish sighed and sat down. He towered over the spaniel and possum, even while sitting. "I lost my people. They moved away without me."

"Please," said Scout. "You scared everyone on Montagu Street in just a few weeks before your people moved away. You had plenty of chances to make friends. Instead, you chased and bit everyone!"

"You never invited me to a Dog Party," accused Hamish.

"You didn't give me a chance. You bit my ear and tried to swallow my head!"

Hamish said nothing and hung his head.

Chisolm said, "Well, if you miss your people, go find them."

"I don't know how."

"You shouldn't stay here," said Scout.

"Why not? I'll be good and not bite anyone."

"Or create havoc and blame it on Scout?" asked Chisolm.

But Scout said, "Maybe there is a way to return Hamish to his family."

CHAPTER 7 – THE PLAN

A few days later, Scout had an idea. An interesting and bizarre idea.

"Chisolm," he whispered into the darkness of his back yard as he sat on the wooden steps. He was taking his last let-out before bed.

"Hello," said Chisolm immediately. He sounded close by.

Scout started. "You scared me!"

Chisolm ambled into the light emanating from the back door. Once again he'd been sitting in the rosemary bush beneath the kitchen window.

"I think I have an idea about how to get Hamish back to his family!" said Scout.

"Really? How?" Chisolm was chewing on rosemary spines.

"My mumma might shop at Will's store at the same time as Hamish's mumma. Maybe we can put Hamish into my mumma's purse. Then, he can get into his mumma's purse at the store!"

"Well, that's certainly interesting," said Chisolm. "What kind of purse do you think would do?"

"What do you mean?"

"Well, there are all types of purses. Cloth, plastic, metal, any material you can think of. He's a ghost, so some restrictions may apply." Crunch, crunch.

Scout had not considered this angle of the plan. He wondered if Hamish would know what type of purse he would need.

"We could ask him," suggested Chisolm.

"How do we find him?"

"Oh, let me try." Chisolm turned and called into the darkness, waving a rosemary sprig, "Hamish! Here! Now!"

And Hamish appeared. He leaned over the pair as they explained their plan.

Hamish was doubtful. "I don't know anything about purses except how they taste. I've eaten or taken a bite out of almost every one my mumma had and she had a bunch. So maybe we should try a solid kind, a plastic or metal one. They were hard to eat. I did enjoy the leather ones, though."

He sighed and then suggested: "What if I moved in here with Scout? He has two ghosts. I've seen them. I'm lonely over there by myself."

"No way!" said Scout.

But then Scout had a thought. "Maybe you could stay for a while and scare my ghosts away."

Chisolm whispered, "I think this is a bad idea."

Scout ignored Chisolm.

"OK, Hamish. You can come in my house and scare away my ghosts. Then I'll make sure mumma chooses the right purse when she goes shopping so you can be in it and get back to your mumma."

"Well, what if the ghosts won't go away?" asked Hamish.

Scout was certain Hamish could frighten anyone and anything without even trying. But instead he said, "Fine, then you have to take my ghosts with you."

Hamish said, "I can't make any promises like that. I've never met these ghosts. What if they're difficult?"

"Oh, like you?" asked Chisolm.

CHAPTER 8 – THE GHOSTS

Chisolm went back into hiding and snacking on palmetto bugs under the rosemary bush as Scout pawed the back door. His mumma let him in, along with Hamish, and they went upstairs to bed. Mumma and Dad read in bed for a while, then turned out the light. They hadn't an inkling they had admitted a ghost dog bully into their house.

Scout rested in his dog nest on Dad's side of the bed. Then he went into the hall. Hamish was sprawled on the third floor landing.

"Wow. Guess what!" said Hamish.

"What?" said Scout.

"You wouldn't believe what's on the third floor in your mumma's studio."

Scout cringed. It never occurred to him there might be more ghosts, or something worse.

"What did you find on the third floor?" he finally asked, not really wanting to know the answer. He knew Mumma's studio; it was a dull place where she attempted to paint. She had an easel, some tubes of oil paint and a bunch of canvases. It was hot up there and smelled bad. Scout avoided going in there if he could.

"A whole bunch of cow bones in a closet! I bet they're tasty!"

The holiday decorations also lived on the third floor, Scout remembered.

"Oh, those," said Scout. "Those are just Halloween decorations. I tried them once and they're all dried out. No flavor whatsoever. Have you seen my ghosts yet?"

"No. So now what?" asked Hamish.

Scout had planned ahead. He had chosen a purse he thought might do the trick of containing some ghosts.

"I've chosen that antique brown Lucite purse with a

latch. What do you think?" He nodded towards Mumma's dresser. She used the purse often since it was a new purchase and described it to everyone.

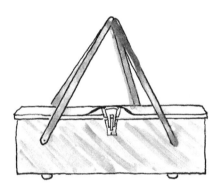

"Looks OK to me," said Hamish, not much interested.

"OK, so let's find some ghosts."

They sat and waited. And waited.

Scout was nodding off to sleep when the pair of girls wandered into view from the guest room.

Scout started. This was really starting to be scary.

He'd never tried communicating with them, and now he said, "Hello?"

Hamish automatically growled.

The girls, dressed in long lacy nightgowns, screamed when they saw Hamish.

Scout waited to see if they disappeared. He hoped they would.

They stopped screaming and the taller one said to Hamish, "We know you. You're that mean dog from next door."

"Really?" said Hamish, flattered.

"Yes. You've been saying mean things to Scout here." The shorter one tried to pat Scout, but her hand went right through him.

"Yes," said the other. "Being fluffy is wonderful, not stupid. You're just jealous since you have wiry hair."

"Oh," said Hamish, rather sadly. "Aren't you scared of me?"

"Surprised, not scared."

"OK, well, you have to leave now," said Hamish.

"Why?" said the older.

"Where would we go?" said the younger at the same time.

"We live here," continued the older.

Hamish said to Scout, "See, I told you this was silly. They're not afraid of me and they're not going anywhere."

"Oh no." Scout said, "This isn't going as I planned." He said to the girls, "You scare my people, so I want you to go away."

"Why?" repeated the older.

"Where would we go?" said the younger at the same time.

"We live here," repeated the older.

Scout thought for a moment. "How would you like to visit Hamish's people? Like a vacation?"

"Why?" said the older.

"Where would we go?" said the younger at the same time.

"We live here," continued the older.

Scout gave up.

Hamish said, "See, I told you this was a dumb idea."

"OK," said Scout. "You're right. You'll have to ride in the purse alone when we go shopping –"

"SHOPPING?" chorused the girls. "You didn't mention shopping before. We'd LOVE to go shopping! We haven't been shopping since before the War Between the States!"

They clapped their hands soundlessly and jumped up and down.

Oh no, thought Scout. He didn't have a good feeling about this now. He wondered if they would all fit in the purse.

CHAPTER 9 – SHOPPING

That day, Scout's mumma prepared to shop. She put on a cool dress, lipstick and sandals.

Scout had already opened the purse with his nose and helped the girls inside. He had hidden Hamish in her purse earlier that morning. Now when Mumma picked it up to leave, it felt as if it had been in the fridge. The inside of the purse also appeared a little cloudy. Scout hoped no one lost an arm or a tail with the opening and closing of the lid.

Scout bolted out the front door to the gate and sat down, hoping he was included in this trip.

He was relieved when he saw his mumma gather some plastic bags from the ceramic frog planter and his leash. The planter formerly housed a purple bushy flower that had died immediately.

She attached his leash to his collar, locked the gate, and away they went.

Scout watched the purse as they walked down Montagu Street toward King Street. The resin was almost transparent and he could see the ghosts swirling around inside next to Mumma's lipstick and credit cards.

But they didn't go straight to Minimum Will's store. First they stopped at another store where Mumma tried on many pairs of shoes.

"Fabulous purse!" exclaimed the salesman.

"Yes, isn't it interesting?" said Mumma. She demonstrated opening and closing the lid. "I bought it at an antiques store on John's Island."

"Oh, I know the one," he said. "That's a fabulous store. Most of my living room came from that antique mall."

"I think it's Lucite, 1940's."

"I agree. Now, how 'bout these cowboy boots?"

Mumma sat down to try them on.

Then the purse began to rattle and the latch opened. The girls peeped out and then flew up and out into the store. Hamish stuck his head out.

"Whew," he said. "This is really a drag. I am sure glad my mumma never took me shopping. Because she shops a lot!"

Scout said, "We've got to find those ghosts!"

"Why?"

Scout thought for a moment. Indeed, why? He scratched his head with a back paw. They were out of his house and happy to be shopping.

So he waited for Mumma. And waited and waited. Two hours later she decided to buy nothing and they went on to Will's store, finally.

The store was packed with people, mostly women. Mumma was looking at jeans when SallieLou appeared at her elbow and poked her.

"How you? I haven't seen you in forever!"

The two ladies were pleased to see each other and hugged. Purses were set down on a sweater table and clothing options were compared.

Meanwhile, Carla and Will rushed over to Scout.

"Scouty!" said Will.

Scout rolled on his back and waved his paws in the air. Other customers smiled and stopped to pet him.

Carla produced a cookie from her pocket for Scout. He enjoyed his cookie while she scratched his tummy. Carla and Will went back to work and Scout watched Mumma look at clothes. He wondered if should help anyone accessorize with a belt or scarf.

As Mumma and SallieLou shopped together and caught up on local gossip, Scout took this opportunity of being unnoticed to nudge SallieLou's purse closer to Mumma's purse. He worried that SallieLou's purse might not hold Hamish. He might have a difficult time staying in a floppy leather bag. It seemed to have a hundred pockets and a hundred shiny gold buckles and zippers all over it. The purse itself was a luminescent greenish gold. Hideous, thought Scout.

He noticed one of the pockets was open and he nudged Mumma's purse. The latch was still open.

" Hamish! Now's your chance!"

Hamish rose from the honey-colored purse like a wisp of chilly smoke and funneled himself into the purse's pocket.

"How is it?" asked Scout.

"It's OK, I think. I hope I can hang on in here."

"What will you do if you can't?"

"No idea. Move into this place?"

Scout dreaded that idea. He wanted to have fewer scary things in his life, not more. If Hamish lived here, Scout wouldn't be able to avoid him when he came to the store.

"Well, if her purse doesn't work out, I'm sure you can find your way to their new house?" Scout was hopeful Hamish would improvise.

"Or I could move back to your house."

"Well, you might as well stay at your old house if you're not even going to try!" Scout was becoming frustrated with Hamish's negative outlook on the current situation.

Just then, Hamish's mumma returned, frantic that she

had left her purse sitting on a table. She was pleased to find Scout guarding the purses. Now she patted him and said, "Good dog! See you later, Scout!"

She picked up her purse and took her new clothes to the register. Scout stayed with his mumma's purse, but he wished he could go behind the counter to be patted and eat dog cookies.

Mumma wandered back, looking absent-minded. "Oh, there you are. And there's my purse! Good Scout!" She patted him and he wanted to roll over and wave his paws in the air, but he wanted to make sure Hamish stayed in the purse and left the store.

He followed Mumma to the register. Carla was happy to feed Scout a cookie.

SallieLou hurried out the door with, as far as Scout knew, Hamish tucked in a side pocket of the ugly shoulder bag.

Scout and his mumma were walking out the door when they saw SallieLou tussling with a young man on the street. He grabbed her purse and yelled, "That's my sister's purse! It's one-of-a-kind! Let go!"

CHAPTER 10 – THE LOST PURSE

The man raced away, around the corner with SallieLou's purse.

Scout didn't know what to do except chase after him. He bolted from his mumma, the leash flying out behind him. He knew he had to be sure not to get it caught on a fire hydrant or something. He knew he could wriggle out of his collar if things became really desperate. His mumma called his name frantically.

"Scout! Scout! Come back here, Scout!"

But he knew he had to save that purse to make sure Hamish went home with SallieLou.

As Scout rounded the corner onto Hassell Street, he saw no one. The street was empty.

Scout sniffed for clues. Then he peed on a "No Parking" sign. He could hear police sirens coming toward the store and knew he had to get out of sight quickly, or give up and go back to his mumma.

He heard a "Sssst!" coming from a storm drain under a fire hydrant.

He looked down into the darkness and didn't see anyone at first. Looking closer, he realized it was Bea the Boa Constrictor lurking just out of daylight. He had met Bea a few days earlier in the storm drains while searching for Ike and Clyde with Chisolm. She was terrifying. He was sure she could swallow a whole terrier and probably a Springer Spaniel!

"Bea?" he asked.

"Yesss. How are you, Scout?"

"I'm well. Well, sort of. I'm chasing a mugger. Did you see him go by, into a store maybe?"

"Sssss." That was snake for "Hmm."

Scout was impatient and afraid at the same time. "Well, I need to hurry on. Good to see you."

"There, in that rice steamer store. I heard a crash. Maybe he ran in there."

"OK!" said Scout and he dashed over to the window to see what he could see.

In the display window stood an easel with a sign that read, "Charlestonians are like the Chinese. They eat a lot of rice, worship their ancestors, and speak a language that's hard to understand." Scout knew this because his mumma laughed at the sign every time they walked by it on the way to the bank. Scout himself was particularly fond of red rice, rice steamed with tomatoes and bacon.

But he couldn't see anything in the store. It appeared to be closed. Bea must have been mistaken. He wondered how good of hearing did snakes have since they didn't look like they had any ears...

Just then he saw some wharf rats relaxing in the

window with the rice steamers. They looked exactly like the unkind group he and Chisolm had met in the storm drains several days ago. At least they looked familiar in their sunglasses and spiky hair-dos.

Scout went to the mail slot in the door and said, "Hello?"

One of the rats came over and said, "What's up, housedog?"

Scout said, "Oh, you do remember me then. From the storm drains with Chisolm?"

"Yeah. What do you want?"

"Did a man just run in here with a purse?"

"Nah. He tried but we lock the door when we're hanging out in here. Customers are annoying. Anything else?"

Scout said, "No, I need to hurry on. Thanks!"

But he realized he was a free dog, and he could be snatched by a thief or animal control at any moment. He dashed into a parking lot. A tent sale appeared to be happening. Dozens of women were lined up to buy purses. Scout thought maybe the thief had taken the money from the purse and dumped the purse in the pile. Upon closer inspection of the purses, he realized no one would think that horrible purse was for sale with these cute purses. Most of these purses were tiny and had large flowers attached to them. Then, he saw the back door of the store propped open. He scooted inside before anyone saw him.

The store was dark and clothes hung low enough to conceal him. He hid and waited under a crispy sounding formal dress while he observed his surroundings. Sometimes, he'd heard from his mumma, a mugger might casually leave a stolen purse behind, after taking the contents, in a dressing room and walk right out of the store, unnoticed.

Scout thought desperately, "I can't check every

dressing room on King Street! That would take years!"

Then he felt a slight nudge on his back. He turned and came face to face with Ike and Clyde. They were shopping with their mumma. Scout was thrilled to see them. The wonderful thing about King Street was that dogs were welcomed in most stores. The expanded experience made King Street a desirable destination for those with extra sharp smelling senses.

Ike hopped up and down. "Hi Scout! Are you on a rescue mission? Solving a mystery?"

"Be quiet," said Clyde. "No one wants to listen to your yapping!"

"Actually," said Scout, "I believe I am on another adventure." He wriggled under the shiny black dress hem.

"Oh, do tell then," said Clyde.

"I'm after a mugger," said Scout.

"A hugger?" said Clyde. He was a little deaf. "I would imagine you receive plenty of hugs. They probably come to you. Why would you have to go after them?"

"NO!" said Ike. "MMMMugger, you nitwit." He made m-m-m-m noises with his lips.

Clyde rolled his eyes at Ike. Since Boston Terriers have large eyes, he very was good at it.

Scout paused. "I'm checking all the dressing rooms on King Street for an ugly purse. A floppy, iridescent green shoulder baggy thing with pockets and zippers and buckles."

"Oh my," said Clyde. "That sounds awful."

"What a terrible trend. Why would anyone want that back?" said Ike.

"Well, it has something in it the mugger wouldn't see. A someone."

"Who? Who would travel in such an atrocity?" queried Clyde.

"A ghost," said Scout.

The pair gasped.

"Which ghost?" asked Clyde. He knew Charleston was full of ghosts, some of whom he knew personally.

"Hamish."

The pair gasped again.

Then Clyde said, "Good grief. Good riddance! He was terrifying. He bit me, Ike and Mumma! Twice!"

"No no," said Scout. "I really am trying to get rid of him. His people moved without him and I managed to put him in his mumma's purse so she would take him home, far from Harleston Village. But then a mugger grabbed the purse. I need to return the purse to his mumma."

"But if the purse is gone to wherever, then he's gone, so mission accomplished," said Clyde. He looked around the store nervously to make sure no one was watching them plot to save and then banish Hamish.

"I want to be satisfied he's gone," continued Scout. "That purse could end up anywhere, maybe even back in

Harleston Village!"

Ike and Clyde agreed. It was best to be certain that
Hamish was deposited with his mumma.

"Well, we're going to be shopping a lot today, so we'll
check any dressing rooms and stores," said Clyde, as their
mumma led them to a dressing room.

Scout eased out to the parking lot again. All of the
stores on this block of King Street had back doors to the
parking lot. Most of them were wide open on such a
pretty day. It was easy for Scout to zip into one store after
another and check the dressing rooms.

The dressing rooms were usually made of curtains, or,
if they had doors, the doors were short. Scout could stick
his head under the door and sneak a quick peek to check
for the lost purse. He only surprised one lady, and she
laughed at him. The sales people just assumed he
belonged to a browsing shopper since he had on a leash.

They patted him and gave him cookies.

Scout was becoming full, sleepy and discouraged when he found himself in the familiar shoe store. He decided to sniff around while the store was empty. Everyone had gone outside to watch the police look for the mugger.

Scout was standing in front of a long mirror thinking how shoe stores all smelled the same when he heard a loud "BOO!"

He growled. It was the older girl ghost from his own house.

"Goodness, what are you up to?" asked Scout.

"Well, since you never learned my name and just abandoned us here, why should I tell you?"

"How on earth would I learn your names? You never told me."

The ghost appeared to pout.

"OK, I'm Scout. Who are you?" He sat down and scratched his ear.

The younger ghost appeared and said, "I'm Elizabeth. She's Kate."

"Oh. How are you enjoying this store?"

The one who was Kate, the older one, said, "We love it. We didn't have shoes like this for girls in 1856."

"Yes, this is fabulous. See? We already have them on," said Elizabeth. She pointed to her four-inch snakeskin platforms. Kate wore a pair of bright red rubber boots.

"Maybe you can help me," said Scout.

"Sure! Anything! You did us a big favor! Now we can go anywhere on King Street we want!" Elizabeth clapped her hands, though they made no sound when they came together.

"Or at least we think we might be able to," Kate warned Elizabeth.

"I need to find an ugly purse a thief snatched from a friend in another store today."

Kate and Elizabeth listened to Scout's description, growing more horrified by the second.

"No, please, no more."

"What a hideous creature that purse must be!"

"Woe to anyone who sets eyes on it!"

"They'll be blinded for life!"

Scout thought this was a little dramatic. Then again, the purse was indeed an ugly of epic proportions.

"We'll split up and find this demonic purse that contains Hamish, the Scourge of Montagu Street," said Kate. And with that, they vanished.

Scout thought he ought to go back to Minimum Will's store. Mumma would be terribly worried about him by now.

He hadn't gone but a few steps when Kate and Elizabeth reappeared.

"We have found a cursed object that matches the description of the horrid purse," said Kate.

She pointed, solemnly, to a cooking store.

"Beyond the glass barrier, under the cave in the back, you will find it in a small cell."

"What?" said Scout. "That doesn't make any sense."

"It's in the store room in the back, in a desk drawer, you silly housedog," said Elizabeth. "Kate's just trying to sound like a ghost." She shook her head. Kate crossed her arms and pretended to ignore Elizabeth.

"Goodness," said Scout. "Well, many thanks!"

"Good luck," they said and Scout thought he saw them fly back into the shoe store, but he wasn't sure. Ghosts are hard to see in bright daylight.

He hurried into the store which was easy since everyone was still distracted by the mugging. He knew he wasn't allowed in this store since they cooked and sold food. Scout didn't know why, except maybe that anyone could see he could eat all the food in this store in a few minutes.

He passed some wonderful smelling herbs and a fresh cake cooling on the counter. He wanted to taste it but knew time was short. People would forget about the mugging soon and find him!

Luckily, the storage room door was open. Kate was right. Under a desk he could see the purse. But what was the part about being in a locked cell?

Then he heard something. A drawer seemed to shake in the desk. Scout pawed at it. It wasn't locked. He looked inside and was stunned to see an identical purse stowed in the drawer. How could this be?

CHAPTER 11 – THE LOOK-A-LIKE

"Don't just stand there, let me out!" said a familiar angry voice.

"Hamish, is that you?"

"Scout, is that you?"

"Yes! I found you! What are you doing in here?"

"I think I'm in lost and found."

"Oh! What happened?"

"The thief ran into this store and tossed me under the pots and pans shelf area. An employee found it and me and put me in here."

"Why wouldn't they hand it over to the police? They're all on the street right now looking for clues."

"How should I know?"

"Hmm," said Scout. "OK, I'll take you back to Minimum Will's store and he can figure out how to find

SallieLou."

Scout grasped the purse in his jaws and proceeded out to the display floor. Just then, his mumma and SallieLou walked in.

"Oh, thank goodness! Scout! You're OK!" Mumma kneeled down and hugged Scout for several minutes before she noticed the purse. "Look, SallieLou, I think this is your purse!"

"It IS my purse. How weird is that?"

Employees and customers began returning to the store. One of the sales reps raced over to SallieLou and demanded, "What are you doing with my purse! I'll call the cops! Somebody was just mugged!"

"This is my purse. Maybe we have the same purse. And it was I who was mugged!"

SallieLou was very tall and could intimidate people when she wanted. She checked the contents of her purse, and, satisfied it was all there, swung the bag on her shoulder. She placed her hands on her hips.

"I'll, I'll go check my desk and see if my purse is there…" and the clerk rushed off to the storage room. She reappeared immediately with her identical purse.

"Wow, it is the same purse," she said.

SallieLou, Mumma and the clerk laughed.

Mumma said, "Do the police need the purse for evidence?"

"Oh no," said the clerk. "My brother must have thought you picked up my purse by accident. He ran in here earlier and gave yours to me. I didn't think anything about it since I was busy. I figured I'd left it at home and he was just being thoughtful and bringing it to me. I need to make sure he got it straightened out with the police so everything's OK."

She looked worried and rushed back outside.

SallieLou gaped. "I paid an enormous amount of money in New York for this purse! It's supposed to be one of a kind."

"Hmm," said Mumma, looking up at the ceiling doubtfully.

SallieLou touched her purse again. "They must refrigerate the back room. It's kind of chilly!"

While Mumma said goodbye to SallieLou, Scout nudged at Hamish in her purse. "Goodbye and good luck, Hamish!"

"Thank you Scout! You're the best!"

Mumma and Scout walked home. On their way they met Ike, Clyde and their mumma. They talked about the mugging and the look-a-like purses.

"Whee!" said Ike. "We helped solve a mystery! It was fun checking all the dressing rooms. We ran around in all the stores and everyone patted us. Some people gave us dog treats!"

Clyde thought Ike was silly but Scout thanked them

both for their help.

That night, during Scout's last let-out before bedtime, he found Chisolm sitting in the rosemary bush.

"Hello," said the possum. "How was your day? Did you get Hamish into his mumma's purse?" He was nibbling on a palmetto bug. Crunch, crunch.

"Yes, I hope so. For a moment, I didn't think he was even going to try to get into that purse! And then it was snatched, because someone thought it was someone else's and they thought they were rescuing the purse."

"But Hamish is happily on his way, right?" asked Chisolm.

"Yes, as far as I know. And Ike and Clyde helped. They were shopping with their mumma so they searched those dressing rooms."

"What happened to the girl ghosts?"

"Well, I learned their names, Kate and Elizabeth, and they flew out of the purse in the shoe store. Which they love and have no intention of leaving it or King Street ever."

The spaniel and the possum sat in the moonlight and wondered about ugly purses, where they came from and why people were so possessive of them.

"I suppose you carry things in it, like keys. Which are supposed to be important," mused Scout.

Chisolm changed the subject. "So what are you doing tomorrow, Scout?"

"I hope I am going motor boating. But Mumma said something awful about yard work and planting bulbs later. Which means we'll be stuck here all day sweating."

Scout did not like it when they did yard work. It was a dull day. Mumma and dad were very grumpy. In contrast, when they all went motor boating, everyone was very happy.

"Oh, I'll be napping while you do that," grinned Chisolm. "By the way, are bulbs crunchy? Are they tasty?

What do you eat them with? How about a nice garlic broth?"

"NO! You're not supposed to eat them! They're for Mumma's annual Impromptu Tulip Mania Party."

"Oh, my," said Chisolm. "Too bad."

"But it's quite a sight when they all bloom," said Scout.

He was looking forward to the tulip party. Every year his mumma posed him in the flowers and took his picture. Then she used it for the invitation. But most importantly, the tulip party meant lots of kind people who fed him lots of cheese, barbequed pork and rare tuna. All he had to do was lie in the middle of the dining room with his paws in the air. No one could resist such cuteness and fluffiness!

Part III

The Missing Tulip Bulbs

CHAPTER 1 - NEW PUPPY

The next morning, Scout jumped out of his bed and went downstairs with Dad. Dad always brewed coffee before his shower and gave Scout a cookie. Scout knew what to expect every day: a cookie and the smell of coffee.

Scout went outside into the chilly, sunny day; nothing appeared out of the ordinary in his back yard so he batted the back door's screen with his paw and Dad let him back in. But something was amiss inside. Instead of going back to bed to sleep in on a Saturday morning, his people, Mumma and Dad, seemed to be rushing about, getting ready to leave. Worse, no one invited Scout to get in the back of the station wagon and they knew he loved car rides. A few minutes later he was alone.

The house was silent. He took a nap in the living room. The kitchen was drafty in the winter. Usually someone came by to play with him if both of his people left. He didn't have to wait long before Minimum Will, a friend of Mumma's, clomped in, wearing overalls. He carried a large duffle bag that smelled, to Scout, like laundry.

Will stuffed a load of clothes in the washer and said, "Hey, Scouty. What's up?" He was called Minimum Will because he preferred to own as few material things as possible in his very small apartment, so he certainly did not own a washer and dryer. Scout had been to Minimum's apartment several times on walks to pick up or drop off laundry.

Scout hopped up and down next to the front door. Will grinned and said, "Let's go for a walk!"

And walk they did, down Montagu Street to Coming Street, to George Street, and then to Scout's favorite block on King Street, The Dirty Block. Situated between George and Calhoun Streets, The Dirty Block was famous for its many fascinating smells that stained the bluestone sidewalks. No power washer on Earth could clean these sidewalks. Scout could hardly tear himself away and Minimum Will had to keep reminding him to stay focused on the walk.

Scout and Minimum Will were having much fun walking around downtown Charleston. The sidewalks and gutters were a cornucopia of discarded food – pizza slices, bagels, chicken bones. Sometimes Scout got lucky. Other times Will commanded: "OFF!" so Scout had to leave the food alone.

When they got home, Will unlocked the front gate to the courtyard and Scout bounded in, dragging Will with him. Surely his people had returned by now.

"Scout! Wait!" yelled Will, since the leash was wrapped around his wrist.

Scout jumped up the brick front steps, and came face-to-face with… it was hard to say. (Meanwhile, Will was removing Scout's leash.)

The small creature sat between Dad's feet. He was black and white and had little black button-like eyes, eyes that appeared to be uncertain. He reminded Scout of someone. With horror, he sniffed the fuzzy little thing. All of the sudden, he knew, as the timid fellow gazed into Scout's eyes. He knew it was… NEW PUPPY!

Oh no, thought Scout. This can't be good.

Dad squatted down and patted NEW PUPPY's head. New Puppy had a tubby little belly and small head. He looked like one of those baby penguins he'd seen watching the animal channel sometimes on TV.

"Now Scout, this here is Benne Wafer. He's much younger so you have to look after him."

Hmph, thought Scout. A preschooler.

"Let's show Benne the backyard."

Will was excited about New Puppy. "Let me know when I can walk him! He is awesome!" Will went inside to check on his laundry.

Scout, Dad and Benne Wafer all went down the driveway and through the garden gate. Dad carried Benne and set him down.

"Now, Scout, show Benne where to pee! Let's go hurry up, Benne!"

Scout picked Mumma's favorite camellia bush in bloom and whizzed it down. Dad sighed. He knew it would take time for Scout to accept Benne Wafer. He knew Scout was an excellent dog and would do the right thing, eventually, once he got used to having Benne in their home and yard.

"Okay, Benne, let's go hurry up."

Benne looked up at Dad and then at Scout. He plodded around the yard and tinkled a little.

Dad danced and sang and made a big deal out of Benne. Scout began to feel a little apprehensive.

CHAPTER 2 - DOG PARTY

It was another bright chilly day in Charleston, but Scout was comfortable sunning himself on the piazza. He was a black and white Springer Spaniel and had grown a soft winter coat. His black fur was all toasty warm. He never went to the groomers in winter. Trimming his coat might interfere with his ability to swim in the harbor during the winter.

Today was an extra happy day. Dogs were coming over for a Dog Party. Scout looked forward to these get-togethers because his dog friends came over for treats while the mummas and dads chatted and drank refreshments. There was much running, jumping and slobbering (by the dogs, not the people) until the tired dogs squeezed themselves under the rocking chairs. All rocking ceased since ears, paws and tails were underneath the chairs in a jumble. There was fear someone might be pinched.

Tali and Charlie, a pair of extra large Golden Retrievers, were the first dogs to arrive with their mumma.

Scout was a little intimidated by Charlie. He remembered when Charlie had first come to live with Tali. He had been smaller than Scout but seemed to dwarf him overnight. In a way, Charlie did not know his own strength. He was constantly squashing Scout until Tali intervened.

Immediately Charlie shoved Tali aside and tackled Scout. He meant to be good-natured and friendly, but Scout yelped.

"Ow! Stop that, you big oaf!" said Scout.

Charlie had Scout pinned upside down on the brick courtyard.

Tali said, "Off, you beast!" He nipped Charlie's tail.

Charlie sat down and grinned, his big tongue hanging

out of his mouth. "What's up?" he said.

"Good grief, Charlie," said Tali. "Be more considerate. Scout's our host. You can't go around tackling him as soon as you walk in the front gate."

"I'm fine," said Scout. He stood up and shook himself and gave Charlie a lick.

Tali himself had not been thrilled with the arrival of Charlie. All he knew was that his people had been walking around for months saying the dread words: NEW PUPPY.

The first two words every dog learns is NEW PUPPY because he IS the NEW PUPPY. Then he learns other words, such as Aw, CUTE! And his new name.

So when a dog's mumma starts saying NEW PUPPY after he's no longer a new puppy, that means someone else is coming to live with him. And he'll have to share everything, including his mumma and dad. But if there's one thing worse than NEW PUPPY, it was NEW BABY.

Thank goodness no one in their dog party group had heard those awful words. Tali knew he should be grateful it was only a new puppy instead of a new baby. He'd heard horror stories about NEW BABY. When NEW BABY came, sometimes OLD DOG had to go.

It was enough to keep any full-grown dog awake at night.

Scout himself had received NEW PUPPY, Benne Wafer, a month ago and he was exhausted. Mumma and Dad had gone away for a long day, and returned with the dread NEW PUPPY...

Right now, the very small creature was napping in his kitchen crate in preparation for the Dog Party. He kept everyone awake at night, fussing in his crate next their bed, three o'clock in the morning outings, and so on. One of them had to carry the fool down the stairs since he was too little to walk. Mumma resembled an impatient zombie after one month of NEW PUPPY. Especially when it was VERY cold, dark and raining outside when an outing was required.

The usual groups of mummas, dads and dogs continued to arrive. Ike and Clyde, the Boston Terriers. Three more black and white Springer Spaniels entered and those three immediately jumped in Scout's fountain.

The fountain could hold a Springer in each of its four sides, Perrin, Bella and Daniel, but Scout preferred to use the fourth side as a drinking fountain. He'd tried for years to teach them not to wade, but they enjoyed it so much he gave up. Scout led everyone, including the soaking wet guests, down the driveway to the back yard to look for squirrels.

And there he was in the garden: Benne Wafer, The Dread New Puppy. He was tucked into some border ivy, with only his little head showing.

All the dogs rushed over to smell him.

"You're very small," said Tali.

"HA, now I'm not New Puppy anymore!" gloated Charlie.

"Yes, and now Scout can really sympathize with me about new puppies," Tali said.

Benne Wafer was four months old and getting braver by the minute. "Hi! I'm Benne Wafer!" He wiggled out of the ivy and all the dogs ran in circles together.

"SQUIRREL!" said Bella suddenly. The herd of dogs sprinted to the back wall. A team of squirrels stood on the high brick wall neatly out of reach of the Dog Party attendees.

"HA!" said Roman, the largest squirrel and the leader. "You silly dogs! You'll never catch us!" The little bandits sauntered along the top of the six-foot wall, mocking the dogs. The dogs leaped and barked while the squirrels laughed.

Ike, the smallest Boston Terrier, was very fierce. He really disliked squirrels. He wasn't much larger than a squirrel himself and that irritated him. No matter how much food he ate, he still remained smaller than Clyde. And now here was a young puppy that was already almost bigger than he.

"You stay out of Scout's yard!" squeaked Ike.

"Or what?" asked Lola, Roman's crony.

"We'll make you wish you had!" barked Bella.

"Goodness," said Perrin, the oldest of all the dogs and the largest Springer Spaniel. She ambled back to the mummas. She'd merely checked the back yard for food, even though no food had been there in the past. She was certain the mummas had food and she was curious to find out.

Charlie raced around the perimeter of the yard after the squirrels.

"No, no! Charlie! Get out of the tulip bed!" barked Scout frantically.

Charlie just looked at Scout and then at the freshly turned soil, not comprehending.

"You can't run around in there! You'll dig up the bulbs! Mumma and Dad spent three days planting for her Impromptu Tulip Mania Party this spring."

"Charlie!" said Tali. "Come out of there now and stay on the grass!"

Charlie slunk down on the tulip bed, trying to make

himself flat and invisible. He didn't understand. What the heck was a tulip anyway? And why did this cover almost half the back yard? Where was Scout supposed to dig? This dirt was perfect for digging!

So many questions for a young dog, just barely full-grown after being NEW PUPPY.

Charlie couldn't help himself. He rolled in the dirt. And rolled and rolled. Tali ran over and nipped his ear. Charlie followed Tali back to the grass and sat down. Benne Wafer jumped into the tulip bed and began digging, his fluffy short legs creating a giant hole.

Scout ordered Benne out of the tulip bed. Benne, embarrassed, sat on the grass next to Charlie.

"Let's run laps on the driveway," suggested Daniel.

Scout looked at the tulip patch. He didn't see any unearthed bulbs, so maybe things were OK. He was looking forward to the tulip party. Every year his mumma posed him in the flowers and took his picture. Then she used it for the invitation. But most importantly, the tulip party meant lots of kind people who fed him lots of cheese, barbequed pork and rare tuna. All he had to do was lie in the middle of the dining room with his paws in the air. No one could resist such cuteness and fluffiness!

CHAPTER 3 - TULIP RECIPES

"Psst!" said the rosemary bush.

Scout was taking his last let-out before bedtime, along with Benne. Benne was wandering around, already sleepy and forgetting to pee.

A "Psst!" from the rosemary bush usually meant one thing.

"Hi, Chisolm!" said Scout. "What's up?"

"Hello," said Chisolm. The fat possum waddled out from under the sticky green bush. Now he smelled fresh and Christmassy.

"How was your Dog Party? Hi there, Benne Wafer," said Chisolm. "Did you have fun at your first dog party?"

"Hello, Chisolm," said Benne. "Well, everyone was very large, but it was fun."

"Oh, and those rude squirrels mocked us," said Scout. "And Charlie and Benne rolled in the tulip bed. But I didn't see any bulbs dug up accidentally, so I guess they're still buried."

"Oh! I tried a bulb once," mused Chisolm. "A daffodil, I think it was. It was quite bitter. I think it would have tasted better with a lovely thyme and carrot sauce. You know, all pureed. Yummy!"

"No, no," said Scout patiently. "You cannot eat these tulip bulbs. They bloom in the spring and then we have a big party. There's lots of food. It's delicious!"

"Oh," said Chisolm, his eyes wide with anticipation. "How do you get the food? Off the table when no one's looking? Is it outside? Could I partake, too?" Chisolm rubbed his tiny paws together happily. He wiggled his ears and whiskers.

"Usually," said Scout, "it's all in the dining room. All I have to do is lie in the middle of the floor where people can trip over me to call attention to myself. Then, people say, 'Aw, how cute!' and give me food. It's a wonderful arrangement."

"I'll bet," said Chisolm, a bit jealously.

"But I can save you some this year and we can share it later."

"Oh goody! What's on the menu?" Chisolm plopped on the grass to listen. His nose twitched.

"Hmm, usually pork over grits, that might be difficult to carry, the grits anyway. Crackers, tuna, steak, grapes – "

"Will there be cheese?" interrupted Chisolm.

"Of course! How could I forget to mention the cheese?" said Scout. "Blue cheese, cheddar cheese, Manchego cheese, and more."

"Oh, well, then I am looking forward to the tulip party." Chisolm smiled, showing his white pointy teeth.

"Me too," said Scout.

"Me too," pipped Benne, having no idea what he was looking forward to at all. He had been watching Scout and Chisolm talk all this time. He wagged his little tail.

Scout glared at Benne. Such a preschooler, he thought.

Chisolm scooted under the bush when Dad came out to find them. He scooped Benne up by the tummy and checked to see if he had peed. He hadn't, so Dad had to stay outside for another half hour saying, "Let's go hurry up. Let's go hurry up, Benne. Let's go hurry up because I'm tired and I need to go to bed!"

Scout smirked and went inside. He raced up the stairs and got on his round green bed and fell fast asleep. He didn't even wake when Benne had to be taken out at two a.m., four a.m. and six a.m.

CHAPTER 4 - THE MISSING BULBS

The scream cut through Saturday morning like a gas-powered leaf blower. Deafening and paralyzing as it was, Scout managed to race downstairs to see what was the matter.

Mumma stood in the backyard tulip bed, and no bulbs were to be found. Just lots of fresh holes, as if someone came by and plucked each one out by its budding stem. Who could have done such a thing and in such a short time? And why? One thing was certain: a tulip bulb thief lived amongst them…

Mumma was devastated and had to retire immediately to her room for some much needed rest to calm her hysterics. Dad stood glumly, espresso in hand, and shook his head at the destroyed flowerbed. He'd been on puppy duty all night, carrying Benne up and down the stairs and was exhausted. And since he had helped plant the seven hundred bulbs, he was equally devastated.

Benne Wafer was hopping around the yard, trying to find some place to nest and hide. Scout thought he was such an odd little thing, always crawling into tight places behind the furniture to burrow. His latest obsession was trying to wiggle behind the clothes dryer and chew on the wiring. Extra security had been built in to keep the puppy out of the utility room.

And the chewing! Scout had been an average chewer, but this puppy was a tornado with teeth. And he was fast. He could dart into a briefly opened closet door and make off with a shoe or cleaning product before anyone could blink. Mumma spent a lot of time on the Internet ordering bulk quantities of chewable stuff for Benne. The backyard was littered with tennis balls, stuffed and rubber animals, sticks and masonry debris. The animals included a legless bear, a wingless duck and a declawed orange crab.

A kind neighbor had brought plastic flowerpots for him one day, and that was hours of fun for pennies. Mumma was an exceptionally good flowerpot placement kicker. She could hit any target, including Benne, if needed. Scout thought Benne looked silly with his flowerpots, his tiny little body, head obscured by the large black plastic pot, trotting around the porch. They played the game for hours every day, it seemed. Scout huffed and lounged on the Barcalounger, watching the game and feeling left out.

But Scout decided he needed to find these bulbs because the party had been planned before Benne Wafer came to live with them. Scout needed something normal in his life, that party, so he sat on the back steps in the sun until Dad went back inside. Dad didn't have on any shoes and it was still cold in February in Charleston.

Scout went over to the rosemary bush and said "Psst!"

"Psst, yourself," said the bush. Chisolm appeared, yawning. He was not at his best and alert in daytime. Nighttime was his prime time. "What was that horrible scream? I believe it woke everyone in the neighborhood."

"That was Mumma – she's devastated. Look! The bulbs have been plucked from the tulip bed!"

Chisolm scuttled quickly to the tulip bed, concealing himself in a ravaged, half-dead boxwood hedge that bordered the former tulip bed. He examined the ground and the holes. "Yes," he said. "I can see where the holes are. You say they're ALL gone?"

"Well, I can't count that high, but it sure looks that way. I watched for two days while they planted the bulbs and it seems that everywhere they were planted are now empty holes."

"My goodness!" exclaimed Chisolm. "How would they have carried them, that many, in a short time?"

"That's what we need to find out because what if they cancel The Impromptu Tulip Mania Party?" said Scout. He was really starting to worry about the bulbs and the party now.

"No! They wouldn't!" gasped Chisolm. "What about the cheese? They can't cancel the party!"

Just then, Dad reappeared with Benne. He walked down the back steps and put the puppy down in a corner of the yard. "Let's go hurry up, Benne. Please, please, let's go hurry up."

Scout felt sorry for Dad, so he went over to the area near Benne Wafer and peed on an old brick to demonstrate for Benne what was wanted of him. Benne's eyes lit up, and he whizzed on the ground. Dad was excited and patted the puppy and Scout on their heads. "Thank you, Scout. That helps a lot!"

Then Benne wanted to play. He chased around his flowerpots for a while, then a squeaky one-legged duck and then a stick. Still being quite small, he decided to nap behind the air conditioner unit next to the back steps. He wiggled behind it and when Dad decided he'd had enough, fearing chewed wiring and thousands of dollars in damage, he rescued the puppy and carried him inside.

Scout continued to worry about whether the party would still be on. Just in case, he started thinking about how to find the bulbs and replant them.

CHAPTER 5 - BACKYARD INVESTIGATION

They left Scout outside. Suddenly, he was surrounded by squirrels perched on top of the garden wall. Scout disliked squirrels immensely. They made such a racket and smelled bad.

Roman, the leader, taunted Scout in his usual manner. "What's up you silly chunky housedog?"

Scout was ready to retort when Chisolm appeared by his side.

"You there, you uncivilized squirrels! What do you know about our missing tulip bulbs?" Chisolm pointed a stick at the squirrels to command their attention.

"You there," parroted Roman. "Nothing! Why do you ask?"

Scout said, "They were here" - he pointed to the tulip bed with his nose - "and now they're gone."

"Well, I wouldn't refuse a bulb," said Roman. "That's good eating!"

Scout was horrified. Surely they'd just found the culprits. Roman had practically admitted to the crime!

"Did you take the bulbs?" asked Chisolm. He liked to get to the point.

"Wouldn't you like to know?"

"Yes, we would, that's why we're asking," said Scout.

"Well then, no, I did not take the bulbs. SHE did!" And he pointed to Lola who had just bounced out of a tree.

"Took what?" asked Lola.

"The prized and missing tulip bulbs, dear," repeated Roman. "Did you carry off seven hundred bulbs last night?"

"I wish! What a record! I'd like to know who did that!" Lola glanced around the yard below, as if the bulbs might suddenly reappear.

"So it wasn't you?" asked Scout.

"No, you furry spaniel," said Roman. "My family is allergic to bulbs. We only feed our baby squirrels the finest acorns. And this neighborhood is well known for its abundance of superb acorns. We saved well last fall. Everyone is fit and happy. No one goes hungry in my nest."

Chisolm, professional detective that he was, asked, "Then how did you know they planted seven hundred bulbs last fall?"

"Goodness," said Lola. "Aren't you interesting? If I must explain to you: young squirrels need to learn to count, and very high. They must know math in order to gather the right number of acorns to feed a certain number of squirrels for a certain number of days. Then they need to calculate the square footage of the nest, measure a sample of acorns and average the size to determine the number that will fit in the nest. These humans, planting their bulbs, are the final exam every year.

"For two days," Lola continued, "the squirrels carefully watch, count and keep track of the bulbs. It's a simple level one final exam for very young squirrels. The older squirrels were out gathering and measuring."

Scout's mouth hung open and he looked at Chisolm. Chisolm shrugged.

"So, we did not take your bulbs. We like to count how many actually bloom in the spring. Then we calculate ratios and fractions."

"Oh," said Scout. He was embarrassed. He couldn't count to seven hundred. Maybe he should try harder and learn.

The squirrels shook their heads at them and scampered off.

"Well, I guess they told us," said Chisolm. "Who knew squirrels were so math-oriented?"

"I suppose they're experts in physics, too," said Scout glumly. Scout had seen the college students in their neighborhood measuring cars' speed, time and distance every semester for their lab class in physics.

"Now, now," chided Chisolm to Scout. "We're all good at something. I'm an awesome food critic and you're good at being cute and solving mysteries. We'll find those bulbs, replant them and the spring party will go on as planned!

CHAPTER 6 -

NEIGHBORHOOD INVESTIGATION

Mumma was feeling better and came outside to assess the damage to the tulip bed. She and Dad had a meeting and agreed there were no bulbs to be bought in mid-February; even florists would be sold out after Valentine's Day. The party was usually scheduled for the first of March, depending on when the flowers bloomed. Bulbs were purchased in the summer, pre-chilled and planted in late Autumn (in the South, anyway). Weather temperature and rain decided mostly when the flowers bloomed. They preferred cold weather and lots of water. Sometimes a sprinkler was required if it was a dry winter.

But the damage was done and no one had a clue where seven hundred bulbs could have gone overnight. Mumma didn't want to have a party without any tulips, cut or planted, so the party was officially off this year.

Scout and Chisolm were determined to find the bulbs, replant them and have this party. The food, and the happiness of Scout's family of course, meant a lot to both of them.

They decided to check with the keeper of Harleston Village gossip: Pudge the Boykin Spaniel. He lived a few doors down the street.

It wasn't as easy to escape from Scout's house as it used to be. There was a new wall in the back yard where the old one hadn't quite sealed the gap. So when Mumma and Dad went to Sunday lunch, they left Scout on the front piazza. Chisolm simply climbed in a tree and took a nap while he was waiting for them to leave. They locked the gate and headed off to John Street to a French bistro. Meanwhile, Benne napped in his crate in the kitchen.

"Psst!" said Chisolm from up in the tree. "Are you ready?"

"Ready!" said Scout.

Chisolm climbed down to the gate and flipped the latch with his fingers and opened the gate. Scout looked out carefully before he walked onto the sidewalk. Sometimes herds of tourists and dogs might be passing unseen until the gate opened and they were upon them, surprised. Scout had once surprised a Great Dane named Hamish this way and was bitten twice on the ears. Hamish had recently been reunited with his people and was gone from Harleston Village, much to everyone's relief. The new neighbors had no pets.

No herds were coming at them on the sidewalks. A skate boarder passed in the street. A car honked at the skate boarder.

Scout ambled down the sidewalk and Chisolm followed him in the trees. They didn't have far to go. Pudge usually kept watch close to home and today he was sitting in front of his yard's white picket fence with a yellow "Boykin Spaniel X-ing" sign hanging on it. The sign was very official-looking.

"Hi Pudge!" said Scout quickly. He looked around fast. Everyone knew Pudge was supposed to be out and about off-leash, but not Scout. He lived behind a locked gate with a sign on it that said, "Mind the Dog". Scout scooted behind the picket fence in order to conceal himself from the street.

"What are you doing out, you silly housedog?" asked Pudge.

"We need to ask you some questions," said Chisolm from above. He added, "Palmetto bug?" It was always polite to offer a snack and Chisolm carried plenty of palmetto bugs with him wherever he went.

Pudge jumped. "Good grief, what are you doing up there, you big rodent? You startled me! I thought you only came out at night." He looked at Scout. "Questions about what? And no thank you, I do not care for palmetto bugs."

"Do you have any ideas or information about who would take seven hundred tulip bulbs from the ground at my house? They were just beginning to sprout and someone came along and just plucked them right out, one by one."

"One by one, huh," said Pudge.

"Yes, and they were just beginning to sprout," reminded Chisolm.

"Is there an echo out here?" asked Pudge. "What do I look like? The Clemson Extension Agency Gardening Department?" Pudge shook his head. "Even if I saw someone with seven hundred bulbs, I wouldn't particularly notice or care. Now, if it was seven hundred dog cookies or seven hundred chew sticks, now we're talking. And, by the way, I can't even count to seven hundred, so I doubt I would know seventy from seven hundred bulbs…" (Hmm, thought Pudge, maybe I should learn to count higher… But how high?)

"Oh," said Scout, thoroughly depressed now. "We thought you might have an idea."

"Did you check with those squirrels?" asked Pudge.

"Yes, we did," said Chisolm. "And they claim to be allergic to bulbs and would rather use them for arithmetic lessons for their offspring."

"That's the strangest thing I've ever heard," said Pudge. "Counting squirrels!"

"Yes," agreed Scout. "I was quite surprised myself."

"OK," said Chisolm. "What should we do now?" His tail curled around his tree branch.

Scout sat down and thought. He could ask the Boston Terriers, but he didn't think they knew anything about bulbs. Nor would the Golden Retrievers. Scout felt he and Chisolm would have to figure this out.

"Wait!" said Pudge suddenly. "I think I know what we can do."

Scout and Chisolm said, "Wow, OK!"

They waited.

CHAPTER 7 - A PLAN IS HATCHED

"Well?" said Scout impatiently.

"I had it, now it's gone," grumped Pudge. "Doesn't that ever happen to you? Losing your train of thought?"

"Hmm," said Chisolm thoughtfully. "No, I don't think so. What's a train of thought?" He nibbled the palmetto bug.

"Ok," huffed Pudge, ignoring Chisolm. "How well have you searched the backyard and under the house?"

"I'm claustrophobic and scared of the dark," said Scout. "We haven't checked under the house."

"You should definitely look under the house. All sorts of things end up there that nobody knows about. It's very exciting!" said Pudge. They had never seen Pudge so animated. His usual demeanor implied he barely had time for any chitchat at all with anyone.

"I'll do it," volunteered Chisolm. "I often go under the house in the daytime for a nap. I hadn't thought of looking for tulip bulbs under there, though."

"Let's get to work!" Scout was excited, but horrified at the same time of going under the house. He knew it was dark and scary beneath the house.

"Why are you scared of going under the house?" asked Pudge. "Surely it's cleaner than the sewers when you went searching for those silly Boston Terriers."

"I suppose," Scout said, hesitantly. "But we were much younger then, and bolder."

"What?" said Chisolm. "Speak for yourself. I'm as bold as ever. Let's go!"

"WE aren't going anywhere," said Pudge and he sat down in his yard, regaining his usual demeanor. "I have some napping to do. And besides, the kids are coming home from school soon. I have to pretend I'm asleep so I can listen in on their conversations." He trotted off to his piazza and lay down under the swing.

"That shouldn't surprise us by now," said Scout. "But Pudge had some helpful ideas."

"Indeed," said Chisolm.

The pair returned to the house, Scout quickly darting behind trees and shrubs to avoid people and Chisolm following along in the treetops and on power lines.

When they got home, Chisolm climbed down the wall. They'd left the gate open and now Scout butted it closed and bounded up the steps. Chisolm turned the latch on the front gate. He immediately waddled down the brick driveway and was about to bat open the hook and eye clasp on the house underpinning's gate when Scout's family returned form brunch.

"Hide!" said Scout.

Chisolm scuttled under the car and held his breath.

"Hi, Scouty!" Mumma said. She gave him a big hug on the front steps. Dad stopped and patted Scout for a few minutes on his way to unlock the front door.

Scout was pleased they were home and hopped up and down. His people exclaimed what a sweet adorable dog he was. Then he drooped. He knew they were on their way to rescue that silly small creature they called Benne Wafer.

They'd make a fuss in the backyard about how wonderful indeed it was that he peed!

Scout followed them inside and watched as they opened Benne's crate and he came out, stretched and looked at everyone with great big sleepy eyes. Everyone, except Scout, said, "Aw, how cute!"

Dad scooped Benne up under the belly and carried him outside. Mumma gave Scout a biscuit which he gobbled up immediately. Then Scout sighed, followed them outside, and peed on a bush to remind Benne of his duties. Benne followed Scout around for a while and then remembered to pee. A fuss was made, patting and cooing and Benne looked pleased. But Mumma and Dad also praised Scout for being so helpful. Scout felt good. Maybe the little Benne was learning from Scout.

Then the family prepared to go for a walk. Scout's leash was attached to his collar. His leash was black and yellow, like a bumblebee, and made out of line from the boat store. Scout had a habit of nervously chewing through his leashes on walks and this material was un-chewable.

Benne's puppy harness was fastened around his stomach and back so that the leash clipped to his chest.

They set off for Colonial Lake. It was a bright sunny day, perfect for walking. Benne and Scout stopped to sniff everything, Benne paying close attention to Scout's interests. Telephone poles, corners of walls and leaf bags set on the curb for Monday morning pickup were popular marks for Scout. Benne sampled leaves, acorns, suspicious blobs and blades of grass. The family continued on, Dad holding on to Scout and Mumma slowly walking behind them with Benne, whose short puppy legs tried to keep up with Scout's bounding energy. Benne liked to grab a leaf and carry it along with him for a while.

Along the way, they met a fierce German Shepard, two small terriers, and another Boykin Spaniel. Benne was terrified when the German Shepard lunged at his gate, snarling and frothing. The Field Springers on Smith Street weren't much friendlier. Benne wondered if all neighborhood dogs defended their properties with such vigor. Such noisiness didn't bother Scout so Benne thought maybe things were OK and he'd get used to it.

Scout always enjoyed the walk around Colonial Lake. He often saw ducks and seagulls and other dogs. The walk was just the right distance to prepare him for his afternoon nap.

Sure enough, when they returned, after treats were given to Benne and Scout, Dad claimed the living room sofa and Mumma claimed the upstairs sofa. Scout opened the front storm door with his paw and lay down on the porch near the steps. Benne fell asleep on top of Dad.

Scout was about to doze off when an extra loud "PSST" woke him. Chisolm was peeking out of the hedge next to the front steps.

"Oh, hi, Chisolm."

"Come on! Why are you sleeping?"

"Oh, I forgot. Our expedition under the house. Sorry!" Scout scrambled to his feet, full of dread at what might be waiting for them under the house in the dark. He'd never been allowed under there. Usually one of his people crawled in after whatever they were looking for and instructed Scout to stay in the driveway.

CHAPTER 8 - UNDER THE HOUSE

The two friends slunk down the front steps quietly. They were more worried about being heard than seen. Benne Wafer was in the living room and might wake up at any moment. His sleep schedule was unpredictable at best. And then he would wake Dad, who would immediately wonder where Scout was.

They also had to be very quiet under the house as well, as the living room would be directly overhead for most of the area.

"What should we do?" whispered Scout as soon as they were under the house. "Should we dig?" There was enough height for Scout to walk easily, but humans had to crawl on the dirt floor. Here is where they stored house repair supplies like paint and wood. Gardening tools lay in a bundle near the gate. It was cool and smelled like dirt under the house.

"No, let's look around first. Maybe they're just piled up somewhere. Let's ask some passersby," suggested Chisolm.

"What passersby?" hissed Scout with surprise. He couldn't see a thing. His eyes were still adjusting to the dark. "Nobody is supposed to be under here!"

"On the contrary," said a raspy voice.

Scout's eyes finally adjusted so he could see in the dimness. The perimeter underpinning was slatted so daylight lit most of the area.

Three huge brown wharf rats stood before him. They all wore sunglasses and one carried a blue tote bag.

"Who are you?" asked Chisolm.

"We are wharf rats and we heard a story about a billion tulip bulbs stashed around here somewhere so we decided to take a look. That's good eating!" said the tallest rat. He wore expensive-looking sunglasses and seemed very relaxed. Scout wondered how he could see in the dark with sunglasses but decided not to ask.

"Yes, we're on patrol," said the rat wearing white sunglasses.

"You're not supposed to be under here. Mumma hires many pest control people to come to the house often. I should know. I've met them all," said Scout. He'd especially liked the squirrel hunters last December.

"Please," said the rat wearing the mirrored sunglasses. "It's a simple task to navigate around the traps. YOU better watch out, though. I bet you don't know where they are like we do."

"Oh, so you come here often?" asked Chisolm.

"Often enough," said the leader rather sneakily.

"Often enough…?" suggested Scout.

"Often enough to wonder why we bother," said the white sunglasses rat rather politely. "I apologize. My name is Morris. My friends here are Clancy and Margaret. It's too clean under here. Not very profitable for us, I'm afraid. We're just passing through on our way to the house next door. We heard they have a garden and the tomato plants just bloomed."

Chisolm looked around. "Yes, Morris is right, no palmetto bugs for tasty snacks. Very clean under here. How are tomato plants? Tasty?"

"So go away and don't come back," said Scout rudely, ignoring the conversation about tomato plants.

"Is this your house?" asked Morris, changing the subject.

"Yes."

"What the heck are you doing down here when you could be upstairs where it's nice and warm?" asked Margaret.

"Well," started Scout, and then they heard a quick shuffling behind them. A tiny figure darted past them towards the chimneys in the back of the house.

I know that smell, thought Scout, and he raced after the little blur.

The very small animal had squeezed himself into the base of the chimney. Scout sniffed him out. Chisolm arrived behind him, the rats in hot pursuit.

"What is it?" hissed Chisolm. He was quite nervous by now. He thought he knew everyone in the neighborhood and found it distressing that someone devious could be living among them, undetected.

Suddenly, Scout sprang into the corner and said: "HA!" He emerged, holding Benne Wafer by the scruff of the neck. Benne looked scared.

"It's you!" shouted Chisolm.

"SHHH!" said all the rats.

Scout took Benne out to the driveway, shook him, and put him down. Benne tried to dash back under the house, but Margaret, Morris and Clancy blocked his path.

"What are you doing, Benne Wafer?" asked Chisolm, not unkindly.

"Yes, why are you trying to nest under the house?" asked Scout. "Why are you nesting all the time? Behind the washer and dryer, behind the air conditioning unit, other places I don't want to know about…"

"Oh," said Benne and he hesitated.

"Go on," said Scout. He nudged Benne.

"I… I like nesting. It makes me feel safe. I like my crate, too." He looked at everyone with his little button eyes.

"Do YOU know anything about missing tulip bulbs," Margaret asked Benne Wafer.

"Yes, we'd love to eat them," said Clancy.

Scout frowned and said, "They're my bulbs and no one is going to eat them. They're going back in the ground, if we can find them." He was annoyed with the rats, thinking they could just take over the tulip bulbs under his house.

"But what's a tulip bulb?" asked Benne in despair. He was so scared, being questioned by older folks, he thought he might cry.

"Now, don't cry," said Morris. He carefully produced a bulb from his bag. "See? It looks like this."

"Where did you get that?" asked Chisolm.

"Yard next door," said Clancy.

Benne's face brightened. Now he didn't feel like crying. He felt like he could be helpful. "Oh, THOSE…"

"YES," said Scout.

"Oh, I might have taken a few from the yard last week. I didn't know what they were." Benne thought he might cry anyway. "Did someone want them? Do they belong to someone?"

Scout tried to be patient. The rats were laughing and Chisolm was becoming impatient.

"Yes, Benne Wafer. They belong in the ground where you found them. They have to go back. Where are they now?"

Benne was quiet. Then he said, "I stacked them in the corner back there where you found me. It's a cozy nest. I didn't know they were important. They're very comfortable." He blinked at them.

Scout was stunned. "How did you get them all in there?"

"Oh, when we went outside. There's another hole in the underpinning. It's easy when Dad's asleep in the yard at two o'clock the morning." Benne felt proud for a moment, then remembered he was in trouble.

"Well, that explains everything," said Scout. "You didn't have to pee! You were just trying to be a little pain. You've wrecked the entire Tulip Mania Party. It's been canceled because of you!"

Chisolm was ready to scold Benne Wafer too, but stopped when tears ran down Benne's little face.

"I didn't know. I've only been here a few weeks. I did have to pee the first few times, and then it became a game. I'm sorry. How can I fix it?"

"Hmm," said Scout, looking at Chisolm. "We'll have to help you think of something."

CHAPTER 9 - REPLANTING THE BULBS

Before Scout had a chance to think, Dad came down the driveway and found Scout and Benne Wafer sitting in the drive staring at each other. They looked suspiciously dusty. Naturally, the rats and Chisolm had all quietly disappeared under the house.

"What are you up to, you two," said Dad. "You're both filthy!" He shook his head and picked up Benne Wafer before the puppy could scoot off and hide in a bush. He left Scout outside and washed Benne in the kitchen sink. Scout didn't fit in the kitchen sink so he was bathed later in the courtyard with the hose. And it was chilly! Scout remembered back in the days when he fit in the kitchen sink as a New Puppy.

Later that evening, while he lolled on the rug in front of the living room fire, Scout had an idea. He would tell Benne Wafer to put the tulips back the way he'd got them out. Even then, it could take a long time. Scout was pretty sure all the bulbs were under the house. If Benne Wafer replanted the bulbs alone, it could take all summer. The bulbs would shrivel up and there would be no party. The bulbs had to be replanted all at once, fast and soon. They needed help.

Scout thought about helping Benne at early morning intervals with Benne pretending he had to pee. But he thought Dad would notice if they were dirty every morning when they got up.

No, this would have to be a group effort. Dogs would be needed to help. Maybe the wharf rats could be bribed, maybe even the squirrels. After all, the squirrels needed the tulips for arithmetic problems for their little squirrels. Scout wasn't sure what the rats would want. Party food? He thought the rats would attract attention at a party. Chisolm was as risky a guest as he could handle. And what if the wharf rats brought friends and family? Scout couldn't very well come up with a contract and party invitations. Scout decided not to ask the rats for help. It was too risky.

So many problems, but then Scout had a thought. He knew there would be a dog party tomorrow on Saturday. Mumma especially liked to invite dogs over often to exercise the puppy. Everyone knows a tired puppy is a good puppy.

During his last let-out for the night, Scout explained the plan to Chisolm and Benne Wafer. Dad trusted Benne to be outside alone with Scout in charge. He could see Scout prevented Benne from hiding under the house that day.

"Chisolm!" called Scout.

"Yes?" Chisolm was reclining in the fig tree by the new wall.

"I have an idea," whispered Scout.

"About the party?" Chisolm's whiskers twitched. He hoped this was good news and a good idea.

"Yes. Benne will have to go under the house and retrieve the bulbs during the dog party. Then we have to replant them."

"That's a lot of bulbs," squeaked Benne fearfully.

"Be quiet," ordered Scout. "You created this mess and now it's going to take all of us working together to fix it."

"Oh," said Benne in a small voice. He sat down to wait and listen.

"All of us?" asked Chisolm.

"Yes, at Dog Party tomorrow, while the people are on the porch, we can get the bulbs and put them back in the ground. The holes are still there. We just need to pop them back in and cover them up. And then pray for cold weather and rain."

"What do you need me to do? I can't be out in broad daylight. Someone will call the emergency exterminator. Or worse, a kid with a pellet gun." Chisolm shivered.

"I need you under the house helping Benne get the bulbs to the opening under the back steps where he went in to stash them. Then the dogs and I will replant and bury them."

"Hmm," mused Chisolm. "Good idea, Scout. I think the smaller dogs would be helpful, like Ike and Clyde. Charlie and Tali are so big they'll just dig the whole place up accidentally by turning around and around."

"I could do it," Benne said in his little puppy voice.

"No, you know where they all are under the house. You're to get under there and hand them to Chisolm who will place them under the steps. And don't you get distracted and go nesting," said Scout sternly. "Chisolm is supposed to keep you focused on the task. I'll carry them to Ike since he's even smaller than Clyde, who will carefully replant them."

"Sounds like a plan, man," said Chisolm. "I think I'll go look for some palmetto bugs now." He hopped on to the neighbor's roof and vanished into the night.

Scout slept well that night on his round green bed. Surely his plan would work and the party with the most excellent food would take place. It was the social event of the season and the guests would be disappointed if they didn't receive invitations.

CHAPTER 10 - DOG GARDEN PARTY

As usual, Charlie and Tali were the first to arrive. Scout knew the other three Springers were out of town with their mumma so that left him waiting for Ike and Clyde before explaining the situation and plan in the back yard. Luckily, no squirrels were to be seen.

"How come we don't get invited to Tulip Mania?" asked Charlie. "Why should we help?"

Scout certainly did not expect this question, but Tali answered Charlie, "Because he's our friend and has fun dog parties. Benne's our friend too!" He swatted Charlie with his big golden tail. He licked Benne on the head who was tucked into the ivy again. Benne wiggled and his little tongue hung out of his mouth.

"Oh," said Charlie. "I'm sorry." He wagged his tail in apology.

"What can we do now, Scout?" asked Tali.

"Mainly keep watch for people. Let us know if they're coming this way," suggested Scout. He felt they would be safe from discovery at least for a while.

The mummas and dads did exactly as they were expected and went immediately to their rocking chairs. There they stayed for most of the dog party until Tali and Charlie had to raise an alarm by barking and running in circles for the team. There was a brief panic before the plan started when Dad stepped into the back yard to make sure the water bowl was still full for Scout and his friends. Benne scooted out from under a hedge so he could be seen and Dad seemed satisfied all was well. He went back to the piazza.

Ike was very puffed up with his new responsibility. Clyde was amused by Ike's enthusiasm, but ready to assist Ike who would be the key gardener, being the smallest dog with the smallest feet. Ike couldn't wait to get started.

"Are we ready yet? Are we ready YET?" He hopped up and down.

Scout nudged Benne and Benne trundled off to his secret opening in the underpinning. Chisolm was ready and waiting beneath the house.

Benne went to his pile of bulbs. The pile was bigger than he remembered, but he gathered as many as he could in his mouth and took them to Chisolm, who ferried them to the back steps. Scout gathered them and deposited them in the boxwood hedge. Ike dashed from the hedge with the bulbs and popped them into their former spots and quickly scattered dirt over each one. He moved so fast he was a blur. He was ready for the next batch before it arrived. Scout was impressed with his plan's execution so far.

"What the heck is going on here?" asked a voice from above. Ike just about jumped out of his skin. "What are you doing?"

Roman and Lola stood on the wall, looking on with great interest.

"Gardening," said Clyde.

Ike continued to move quickly.

"Oh, you found the bulbs," said Lola. "Goody! We look forward to those every year. How many have you planted so far? We'll keep count."

"About twenty-five, I think," said Scout.

"Well, then, only six hundred and seventy-five to go," said Roman. "Lola, grab the kids so they can count."

Lola scampered off and reappeared with two tiny squirrels holding an acorn each. "This is Bridget and Sean. Count, children," she commanded. The little squirrels squinted at Ike and started whispering, "Twenty-six, twenty-seven, twenty-eight, twenty-nine..."

Ike was a whirlwind. His little feet danced and scattered. He left no footprints. He felt wonderful and important.

Meanwhile, Benne was becoming dustier and dustier. He sniffed and his button eyes became a little irritated as he stirred up dust walking back and forth carefully with the bulbs to Chisolm. But he didn't damage any of them. They were all in one piece. Finally he reached the end of the pile. He was so tired he thought he'd take a nap amongst the paint cans. They were piled up like a small fortress. He could just snuggle up in there for a few minutes...

"Hey!" said Chisolm. "Good job, Benne! We're done. Ike says the squirrel counters reached seven hundred. We're saved!" He danced in the strips of dusty sunlight in anticipation of tasty party food in the near future.

Benne Wafer could hardly keep his eyes open. He squeezed out from under the back steps into the bright daylight. Scout gave him a big lick on the head. "I'm proud of you, Benne Wafer." Benne beamed and wiggled.

Scout was proud of all the dogs and they ran around the backyard for the rest of the party, barking and rolling.

When the people collected their respective dogs, they noticed Ike, Scout and Benne were quite dirty. Mumma washed Benne in the sink. Scout and Ike were bathed in the courtyard. Luckily it was a warm winter day in Charleston. Scout hoped Spring would come soon.

CHAPTER 11 - RAINY DAY PUPPY

The next few days were hard on the family. It rained. It was cold. Winter had returned. The puppy grew and gained energy equal to a neutron bomb. He bounced and chewed and barked.

Everyone was exhausted, except for the puppy. Mumma played endless games of flowerpot on the front piazza with Benne Wafer. Scout was worried they'd wear through the floor soon and then where would they be?

Benne Wafer stopped asking to go out at night every two hours, so that was a good thing. Everyone got more rest at night. Occasionally Benne Wafer had the urge to wake everyone at two a.m. to check on the bulbs, but resisted. He knew Scout would be angry with him.

After four days of Rainy Day Puppy, the sun came out. It had been gone a long time and had decided to return. After breakfast the dogs burst from the back door with excitement. Rain always brought new smells. And springtime seemed to be showing signs of staying.

Mumma walked out with the dogs. Out of habit, she studied the tulip patch. Something was growing there! It wasn't greenery leftover from last year's bulbs. They were truly strong green stems with buds. It was a miracle. How had this happened? And how had Benne stayed out of the tulip bed when he dug up the yard and chewed on all the other plants constantly? Hmm, maybe there would be an Impromptu Tulip Mania Party after all.

Mumma went inside to prepare a menu and a list of guests. She made a note to buy a bag of soil to fill in the holes Benne had dug in the yard. No one needed to trip in those during a party.

During Scout and Benne's last let-out before bedtime, they once again found Chisolm in the fig tree.

Scout said, "Chisolm! We did it! The party is next week. Loads of food. And, it will be easy to get food to you this year. They're planning a seafood table outside. With a long tablecloth! You can simply conceal yourself under there!"

Benne hopped up and down and barked in excitement.

Chisolm was thrilled. They had worked hard and the results were successful. "Will there be cheese?" he asked.

"There will be cheese," answered Scout.

"What's cheese?" asked Benne. He'd grown a lot in the last month. His paws were huge on the ends of his slender legs. He could jump straight up in the air and do a little twist when he felt particularly energetic. When that happened, Mumma resigned herself to yet another walk, an hour of fetch and an hour of flowerpot. She mumbled something about how puppies sleeping a lot was a big lie and not getting any client work done.

It was true: Benne never slept. He was all go from sunup to sundown. She told Dad every morning, "Look closely when he first wakes up. That is the only time of day he isn't moving."

And when Dad came home, Benne immediately took a nap so Dad didn't believe a word Mumma said about Benne's excessive energy level.

Scout was tired too. Benne wanted to play all day. Sometimes Benne ran around in such a frenzy even when he was tired, Mumma put him in his crate to calm him down.

Benne looked forward to the Tulip Party until he heard that he was going to be on a leash the whole time and Scout could roam free. Benne Wafer pouted.

"They don't trust me," he said sadly.

"Of course they don't, you nincompoop," said Scout. "You counter surf and run off with everything in your mouth."

"You shouldn't call me names," said Benne sadly. He couldn't help himself. In particular, Mumma's bike shoes were the most fascinating things he'd ever seen in his puppy life! The shoes had Velcro straps that he could stick and unstick, over and over. He could fit his whole head inside the shoe. He could take the strap in his mouth and shake his head, flopping it back and forth. He could even smack Dad with it while running by him at full speed: TH-WACK!

"OW!" yelled Dad.

And her closet was full of equally fun shoes. Every time she opened the door, Benne dashed in and ran off with another shoe.

Then there was the Ritual of the Sock every morning with Dad. Dad sat down with a pair of socks and a pair of shoes. Benne's head spun from excitement. He had to decide which sock to run away with! Whatever sock he left with Dad, Dad put on that sock and that shoe. Then Benne slowly crept back to Dad, trying to decide if he should hand over the sock yet, or run around the entire house with it first. Usually he ran around the house for another ten minutes with the sock. Dad would wait patiently or put on a belt or tie while waiting for Benne to slow down. When he sat down again with the other shoe, Benne knew he must return the sock. And that was how most mornings went with Benne and socks.

Scout wondered if Benne would ever outgrow the Ritual of the Sock. Benne was truly the most playful puppy Scout had ever met.

CHAPTER 12 -

THE IMPROMPTU TULIP MANIA PARTY

The tulips grew quickly, almost overnight. This was why the party was impromptu. The tulips were literally here today, gone tomorrow. The party had to be given immediately when the tulips bloomed.

Mumma posed Benne Wafer and Scout in the patch of flowers and created her annual invitation. The party date was set for three days after the invitations were sent to guests.

You're Invited to the Impromptu Tulip Mania Party!

Scout and Benne greeted all the guests together with Mumma and Dad. Benne discovered even if he was on a short leash, he could still stretch out his long legs and try to give the next nice person a hug. After all, most of the guests hugged Benne and Scout. Why couldn't he hug them back? But the rules, and Scout, suggested he sit and be patted. No leaning or hugging by puppies was allowed.

Scout was not disappointed by the generous handouts from the guests. He was especially pleasantly surprised to discover a plate of tuna left on top of a cooler completely uncovered. He cleaned that plate quickly! Someone found the empty platter and alerted Mumma, who had to make sure it hadn't been covered in plastic wrapping. Scout thought that was silly of her to worry about a thing like that. He would never eat plastic. He would have carefully pulled it off the platter with his lips.

Meanwhile, Chisolm was hiding under the outside table's tablecloth. Scout decided to check on him by walking around to the back of the table.

"Are you getting anything good?" asked Scout.

"Oh, my yes! Shrimp, oysters, clams, cheese! These people are wonderfully clumsy. Those tiny plates make it easy for them to spill everything!" Chisolm sat in a pile of shells, napkins and plates and grinned.

Scout was pleased his friend was enjoying the party so much.

So were the guests. The tulips had survived Benne Wafer and bloomed in record numbers. The guests admired the flowers while they chatted and sipped.

Mumma and Dad were thrilled with the flowers after such worry. Benne Wafer was fascinated by all the people and had to say hello to everyone. Scout noticed his new little friend was well-liked by everyone, just like Scout.

The party was a huge success. The yard was cleaned and everything put away when another springtime shower rolled in. At Scout and Benne's last let-out, they talked about the party with Chisolm some more until Mumma called them inside. She had a beach towel to dry them off. While she was drying Scout, Benne escaped and sprinted up the stairs to find Dad who'd gone to bed to read. Scout felt sorry he couldn't help Dad now. Even Mumma suspected what was going to happen next.

They heard a "Splat!" and a yell from Dad. Even from downstairs Scout could just envision the cold, soaking wet puppy standing on Dad's head in the warm dry bed.

Needless to say, Benne Wafer was pleased with himself. He sat on Dad's head and Dad rolled him into a ball and all four Benne's legs stuck straight up. Benne was grinning happily. He thought he'd found a new place to sleep.

Mumma and Dad did not agree with Benne. They dried him off and placed him in his crate but left the gate open. Scout lay down on his beanbag bed, but was soon joined by Benne after the lights went out.

"Scout?" asked Benne.

"Yes," said Scout. What could the little one want now?

"I'm chilly. Can I sleep with you for a while?"

"I suppose," said Scout. Benne hopped in and together the two-dog pack slept through the night, dreaming about next year's Impromptu Tulip Mania Party. Maybe Benne would even be off-leash and could greet everyone properly!

PART IV

<u>The Curse of the Carriage Mule</u>

CHAPTER 1 - THE FARMERS' MARKET

Scout and Benne Wafer were a bit sleepy the next day, which was a Saturday. The night before had been eventful. They always enjoyed a good party and The Impromptu Tulip Mania Party was the event of the season.

So the two Springer Spaniels plodded down the stairs with Dad to make coffee, have a cookie and check out the back yard. Nothing appeared amiss so they went back inside to find out what the day held for them. Chisolm the Possum was out of sight and napping for the day and the squirrels were probably still asleep. They usually made a clamorous racket, scampering about, on the metal roof of the house.

Dad was gathering shopping tote bags and that usually meant one thing. They were headed to the Farmers' Market in Marion Square. Scout hopped up and down excitedly and was told to stop hopping up and down like a pogo stick.

Benne Wafer, still a puppy, asked Scout, "Why are you so excited? What are we doing?"

This was Benne's first year so he had not been to the Farmers' Market yet.

Scout explained, "It's a wonderful place full of food, people and other dogs. And it's a long walk so we get to smell a lot of things on the way."

Benne was excited now too. He loved meeting new people and dogs. Plus, walking anywhere near King Street always meant lots of food in the gutters and on the sidewalks: bagels, pizza, chicken bones. Their friend Chisolm always raved about the city, calling it a cornucopia of good food and fortune.

Dad clipped Benne and Scout into their harnesses, grabbed his tote bags and away they went. Mumma was off doing some other kind of shopping and errands.

It was a nice cool day in April and they slowly made their way the six blocks to Marion Square. Squirrels chattered and mocked them from the power lines. It seemed to Benne that more squirrels than ever lived in Harleston Village. Benne and Scout sniffed grass and trees.

Scout agreed. He never went anywhere on the street where he didn't see packs of the little bandits running up and down trees, chattering and squeaking.

On they walked. Scout tried to grab a chicken bone and Dad commanded, "OFF!" so he had to leave it in the gutter for some other lucky dog (or possum).

When they got to Calhoun and King Streets, the crowds of people had swelled to such a density that Scout pressed close to Dad's legs. He was afraid of being mowed down and carried off by the mob.

Benne Wafer was enjoying himself immensely. Throngs of people stopped mid-crosswalk to pat him, holding up traffic even longer. Scout was in a hurry to cross the street.

"Hurry up, Benne Wafer," he said.

Benne was being patted by a group of children and he had no intention of hurrying up anything.

The kids moved on and Dad finished leading them across the street. First they stopped at the butcher, then the pasta ladies, and finally at some vegetable stands. The tote bags were full and it was starting to get hot in the sun. Scout and Benne were ready to take a nap at home in the living room. Dad seemed to be taking an extra long time in picking out okra so Benne scooted under a table in the shade and dozed off.

He awoke when the table started moving. Someone was taking it away! Where were Scout and Dad? Oh no, Benne thought. Dad must have had his hands so full he dropped my leash. How do I get home? Will they come back for me?

The table had been folded and carried away by now, so Benne nested in an azalea bush and waited. Maybe his family was nearby and he would see them soon. Then he could just hop out of the bush and they would be glad to see him.

CHAPTER 2 - LOST!

Benne wasn't sure what to do. He'd never been lost. He didn't even know how to ask for directions. He didn't know to whom he should ask directions. Things were becoming a bit confusing quickly. One thing was for sure, everyone at the Farmers' Market was leaving.

He sat down and thought hard. Maybe he could find his way home by some of the things he'd seen on the walk to the Farmers' Market. Maybe he could find the busy road and the smelly sidewalk. And the park. He thought it was a park. Maybe it had been a school. The sidewalks had been brick.

Benne started to move from bush to bush. Hmm. There it was. A big fountain next to the busy road. Herds of people were crossing so he joined in and found himself on the smelly block on King Street. He cheered up. He would find his way home.

Just then, someone picked him up!

"Oh, my," said the someone. "You are a cute Springer Spaniel puppy! Who do you belong to? Do you have a collar? Oh, good," the nice person said, looking at Benne's collar. "You live really close by. I'll just drop you off on my way."

Benne wondered: on his way to where, but he didn't ask. The kind young man whipped out his phone as he walked Benne down King Street. He called Benne's family on the phone and said Benne was safe and the he would drop him off in an hour when he passed their house.

Benne was very curious now. They walked on through the Market Area and stopped at a barn. Benne thought it smelled really funny in there. He sniffed around some while his rescuer went about his business, whatever that was...

"Who are you?"

Benne turned so quickly he spun around on his bottom.

"Oh! I'm Benne Wafer. I'm a Springer Spaniel puppy." He added the last bit because he didn't know to whom or what he was speaking and it sounded better that way, adding on that bit about himself, in case they didn't know to whom or what they were speaking.

"Of course you're a Springer Spaniel," said the horned beast. "Anyone can see that. Pleased to see you, BW. I'm guessing you've never met a Billy Goat?"

"Um, no, I have not." The conversation lagged here.

"That's OK. You're a very young creature so I understand." The Billy Goat had wiry brown hair and had big curving horns on top of his head. Benne wondered what those were for, but it didn't seem polite to ask.

"Are you staying? Are you new? My name is Zip."

"Oh, hello, Zip," squeaked Benne Wafer. He was now surrounded by many animals. Some he recognized, like the mules and horses he had seen pulling carts and carriages. And he saw a big gray fluffy cat. And another goat. The second goat introduced himself as Zap.

All the animals were friendly, except for the cat. He just looked at Benne, not bothering to say hello.

"These horses are a lot bigger up close," said Benne, trying to think of something to say.

"HAH," laughed a rude horse in the back of the barn. It was dim back there, so Benne couldn't see who had laughed at him.

"Oh, don't mind Clementine," said Zip.

"Oh, don't mind me!" sneered Clementine. She came closer and Benne could see she was a different type of horse, but he didn't know what kind and now he felt nervous.

"Hello," he said. "I'm Benne Wafer."

"He's a Springer Spaniel puppy," said Zip.

"I can see that," snapped Clementine. She lowered her great big head with its drooping ears and snorted at Benne.

He was startled and jumped straight in the air.

"For your information," said Clementine, "I am not a horse." Then she walked back to her stall in the back of the barn and into the dimness.

CHAPTER 3 –

CLEMENTINE'S UNFORTUNATE TALE

"Oh yes," said Zap. "She's been telling us that for months now. 'I'm not a horse, I'm a mule' and so on and so forth. Like anyone cares. Mules do the same job as horses, so what's the difference?"

"There IS a difference, but I know you're not interested," muttered Clementine sadly.

"Good grief," said the cat. "Not all this again!" He jumped onto the edge of the stall and flipped his tail at the mule. Then he sat down and proceeded to stare at Clementine. "Go on," he urged. "Tell us this tale of woe. We've been on the edge of our seats for months, ever since you came here."

"Ok, but no interruptions," snorted Clementine. "It was a dark and stormy night," she began.

"Oh please," said Zip. "That's is such a cliché!"

"OK, then it was a hot and sticky day," insisted Clementine. "No interruptions," she reminded them.

"'It was a hot and sticky day' …" urged Benne Wafer. He liked stories and wanted to hear this one before he was returned to his family.

"Yes, as I WAS saying." Clementine glared at Zip, Zap and the cat. She swished her long brown tail and twitched her droopy ears.

"I was shopping on King Street in Charleston with all my BFFs."

"What's a BFF?" asked Benne. "OH, I forgot. No interruptions!" He looked for a place to hide. He slowly backed underneath Zip.

"'Best Friend Forever'," whispered Zip to Benne.

Clementine snorted and pawed her foot. "And we all got out of a cab on Upper King Street for a bit of shopping. We were having a party since my BFF was getting married."

"Married mules?" whispered Benne to Zip.

Zip shrugged. "Shh!"

"And then the unthinkable happened."

The group inhaled sharply.

"Before we could go into the first store, I tripped on the curb and fell face down. But I didn't fall by myself. I accidently fell on a policewoman. I think she was a parking enforcer. And she didn't like that one bit. I've always been a bit clumsy. I was terrified I'd fall down walking down the aisle on the way to the altar. Anyway, she took one look at me, waived her electronic ticket-maker and I was cursed.

"I turned into a mule." Clementine was very sad. "I'd cry but it doesn't help things."

"Did you explain it was an accident?" suggested Benne. He thought the story was over now and he could ask questions.

"Everyone pretends to not understand what I am saying. They called Animal Control and said a carriage mule had escaped. So they brought a trailer and I was put in and brought here. Meanwhile, my friends thought I had vanished. They couldn't believe what they'd seen with their own eyes. I don't know if they even looked for me."

Just then the carriage driver and tour guide came into the barn. They put Clementine in her harness and hitched her to a dowdy wagon. The guide picked up Benne Wafer and put him in the wagon and they drove away. Benne ascertained from the driver's conversation they were going to pick up a private party near his house and he would be dropped off with his family on the way.

Benne was sorry to leave his new friends since he didn't get a chance to say goodbye. But it was exciting to have a ride in the wagon, despite knowing that Clementine was cursed and not really a mule at all. Lots of friendly people waved at him.

"Psst, Clementine," whispered Benne. He sat on the seat next to the driver so he could find out more about Clementine's situation. "Are ALL the carriage mules cursed? I see a lot of mules working all the time."

"I have no idea. But where else would we all come from? But I haven't had a chance to take a poll."

Benne said, "What's a poll?"

"Oh, I forgot. You're a real Springer Spaniel puppy. A poll is a survey; I would ask all the mules if they used to be something else, if I had a chance. I don't get to associate much with the other mules."

Benne thought hard. They turned onto Montagu Street.

"We'll get you turned back into a person," he said suddenly. "I'll get Scout and Chisolm to help me!" He was determined to lift the curse and make Clementine a happy... whatever. Something!

CHAPTER 4 - FOUND AND LOST AGAIN

Benne Wafer's family was overjoyed to see him. Mumma had scolded Scout and Dad a great deal for forgetting Benne at the Farmers' Market.

However, all was forgiven now that he was home safe. They thanked the driver repeatedly and he waved them off, saying, "Benne's an awesome pup. He can come visit the barn any time he wants. I think he got on well and made some new friends!"

He clucked to Clementine and she rolled her eyes in disgust. The driver clucked again and she lurched forward, ungracefully, and the driver had to hang on or fall off the wagon.

Benne watched them go from his front steps. He could see over the courtyard wall from up there. He felt sorry for Clementine. He didn't think he'd want to pull a cart all day either. He was very happy being a Springer Spaniel puppy. People said nice things to him all day long! But he wanted everyone around him to be happy too, and that included his new friend, Clementine.

That night, as they were taking their last let-out before bedtime, Scout, the older Springer Spaniel, asked "Why can't you keep up, you preschooler? Just because Dad dropped your leash doesn't mean you're automatically lost."

Benne wafer said, "Well, it was warm and I was tired so I thought I'd take a little rest under a table. I didn't know you'd be gone so fast! I was swallowed up by a crowd. And then that nice tour guide found me and took me to the barn and phoned Mumma. And then I made new friends. Two goats, Zip and Zap, and a cat – "

"You made friends with a CAT?" asked Scout doubtfully. "I didn't think they had friends."

"Uh, well, this ones lives in the barn anyway. And then I found out about the curse of the carriage mules!"

Now Benne really had Scout's attention. "Cursed mules?" He shook his head. "I never heard of such a thing. How'd that happen?" He sat down in anticipation of a good story. Maybe even a scary story. Scout could believe almost anything was possible after returning a ghost dog bully to its former mumma's purse not too long ago.

"Well, I only met one cursed mule, and she doesn't know if the others are cursed," began Benne Wafer and he retold Clementine's story to Scout.

Scout was amazed. "That's amazing!"

"Psst," said the rosemary bush. "What's amazing? Is it delicious, too?" A fat gray possum waddled out from underneath the rosemary bush. The bush grew directly under the kitchen windows so now the possum was lit up in the dark back yard. He twitched his whiskers happily.

"Hi, Chisolm," said Scout and Benne at the same time.

"Hello," said Chisolm. He nibbled a rosemary spine. "So, what's amazing?" He yawned.

Things had been a bit dull around the house and Montagu Street in general since the tulip party. Chisolm wished they could have a tulip party every week, but it only happened once per year. And this year it almost hadn't happened at all since Benne was such a new puppy, he'd run off with all the bulbs. But the bulbs had been found, replanted, and a wonderful party HAD happened, and with it, lots of tasty food.

"Benne Wafer has discovered cursed mules. Or at least one, anyway. You know, the ones who pull the carriages and wagons all day," said Scout.

"Oh yes, I know of them," said Chisolm, disappointed that amazing hadn't been delicious.

"The curse or the mules?" asked Benne.

"Just the mules," said Chisolm.

"Where can we find out how to reverse or lift the curse?" squeaked Benne. He was still New Puppy and hadn't a lot of worldly experience in such matters as cursed mules.

"Hmm," said Scout. "We'll ask Pudge. He usually knows all about all sorts of things."

CHAPTER 5 - THE CURSE OF THE CARRIAGE MULE

Pudge the Boykin Spaniel was usually a source of somewhat accurate information, even if it was explained in a very roundabout way. He almost never got to the point and never gave a direct answer. Scout suspected Pudge mostly thought out loud, and his advice could be taken several different ways. But Pudge had been correct about the missing Boston Terriers and the missing tulip bulbs, eventually. Pudge's official title was Keeper of Harleston Village Gossip.

The next day was Sunday, and a mild pleasant day. Mumma and Dad left Scout on the piazza while they ran a few errands, carefully locking the front gate when they left. Benne was still too young to be left on his own in the courtyard, so he napped in his kitchen crate.

Scout and Chisolm had a system in place now whenever Scout wanted to visit Pudge, who lived a few doors down. Chisolm scuttled down the tree to the wall and gate. Then he turned the latch and Scout nudged the door open. He carefully peeked around to the outside sidewalk to make sure he wasn't about to be attacked by another dog passing by. The sidewalk was empty so he hurried along from palm scrub-weed to oleander bush to Pudge's white picket fence. As usual, Pudge was on duty. He sat in his driveway on the sidewalk so he could see all activities on his block, everyone coming and going. Nothing escaped his sharp little brown eyes.

"What's up?" asked Pudge when he saw Scout trotting towards him. Scout quickly ducked behind the white picket fence into Pudge's yard. He couldn't be seen by any of the neighbors. They all knew Pudge roamed off-leash, but not Scout. They'd call his mumma and he would be returned to his house, unable to ask Pudge any questions.

Pudge pretended to not like answering questions but he secretly enjoyed being a source of information. And everyone knew him. But he huffed at Scout anyway. He also knew Chisolm was somewhere close by.

"Where's your sidekick, Chisolm?" asked Pudge, looking around.

"Palmetto bug?" offered Chisolm from the tree above them.

Pudge started. "Goodness! You do that every time! Always in a different place!" He glared at Chisolm.

"Oh," said Chisolm. "I didn't mean to startle you, Pudge." He took the offered Palmetto Bug and crunched on it himself.

"Yes, you did," said Pudge indignantly.

"I did," grinned Chisolm, showing his white pointy teeth.

Scout said, "Pudge, what do you know about cursed carriage mules?"

"Let me think." Pudge sat down on the grass in his yard and scratched his curly-haired ear with his hind leg.

"I think it has something to do with meter maids," suggested Scout. He sat down, too.

"Oh, you mean parking enforcers," said Pudge. He was always entertained by the comings and goings of the enforcers, often having verbal disputes with parking offenders. They marked cars and ticketed for all kinds of violations. Even the neighborhood's residents couldn't keep up with the parking laws, as they seemed to change often and quickly.

"Yes," Pudge continued. "I heard they were given magical powers to curse parking violators if they are too resistant to the fine they're given."

"Magical powers?" Chisolm perked up. "How can I apply for the job? What do I get to turn people into? Squirrels?"

Pudge ignored Chisolm and said to Scout, "Have you been cursed by a parking enforcer?"

"Not myself. Benne Wafer met a carriage mule that claims to have been a person and out shopping or something and collided with an enforcer. And thus she was turned into a carriage mule."

"Well, that sounds like a genuine curse to me. And pretty severe for the mistake. Did she mean to flatten the enforcer?"

"I've no idea. Maybe the enforcer was embarrassed and misused the power of the ticketing machine."

"Oh, well, I have no idea how to turn a mule back into a shopper. It's hard to tell which Charleston needs more, a carriage mule or a shopper."

"Can you think of anyone else we can ask?" asked Chisolm. "Who would have the powers to decide if this poor carriage mule should be set free?"

"Hmm, no, but I will keep thinking about this situation," said Pudge. "It's the most interesting thing I've heard all day." He stood up and trotted off to his porch and lay down under the swing for an afternoon nap.

When Pudge was done answering questions, he was done. And he usually stated this by trotting off and taking a nap.

"OK, thanks, Pudge," said Scout.

Scout and Chisolm headed back to Scout's house. No parking enforcers were working today since it was Sunday. No one saw them as they crept down the sidewalk, tree to shrub.

CHAPTER 6 - SCOUT, BENNE AND CHISOLM HAVE A MEETING

When Mumma and Dad returned, Scout was napping on his piazza. They patted him and unlocked the door to rescue Benne Wafer from his kitchen crate. Then Benne and Scout raced into the back yard.

Chisolm sat in the fig tree. "Hi," he said.

Benne and Scout rushed over to see him and barked, pretending to scare Chisolm away. Then they stopped barking and mused on how to solve this important case of identity theft, as it were.

"After all, if someone changes you from one thing to another, that's a sort of identity theft, isn't it?" asked Scout. He heard about identity theft constantly from the radio.

"Indeed," said Chisolm. He yawned and wished they would go away so he could take a nap. Possums napped during the daytime and went out exploring at nighttime.

"Maybe we could find an enforcer or a ticket-maker and turn Clementine back into a shopper," squeaked Benne.

Scout frowned at Benne. "How are we going to do that? We don't know which enforcer it was, and I bet Clementine doesn't know. How long has she been a carriage mule? What if the enforcer has left the city? Where do we get a ticket-maker and how does it work?"

"Oh," said Benne sadly. Those were a lot of questions for a puppy to handle.

"I think one thing is clear," stated Chisolm from above their heads. "I think we should visit Clementine next Saturday and ask her those very questions. Then we'll see what can be done."

"But how do we do that?" asked Scout, confused.

"Do what Benne did last week. Get lost at the Famers' Market. I'll meet you at that horse barn."

"But how will you get there?" asked Benne. "How will you find it?"

"All sewers lead somewhere," said Chisolm, grinning. "What makes you think I don't know every sewer in the city?"

"Yes," said Scout to Benne. "Chisolm is a city sewer expert."

"Oh," shuddered Benne, hoping he wouldn't have to go into a sewer. That seemed awful and scary to him.

And so the spaniels waited for the days to go by, counting them one by one. Certain things happened on certain days. However, certain things may have decided not to happen, so a spaniel could never be sure about the order of the world. Luckily, this week ran on schedule and everything was expected.

On Monday, Miss Wanda came to clean the house. She sang songs to the dogs and let them in and out of the house all day. She let them out the back door and then in. Scout would open the front door so he and Benne could bounce around and bark at enforcers and carriage horses and mules. Then Miss Wanda would let them in through the kitchen piazza door. The dogs went through this routine a dozen times and until they collapsed on the living room floor.

Then on Tuesday the garbage truck came. They never came at the exact same time every week, so the dogs had to be ready all day, if necessary, to be on the piazza when they did come. Who would bark if no one were there?

And the recycling truck came on Wednesday, also never at the same time. The dogs had to be very careful not to miss the recycling truck. It was louder and slower than the garbage truck, so more barking was required.

The mailman also appeared randomly. He was harder to track since he was on foot and quiet.

The package delivery trucks usually came very late in the day. They threw crinkly fun packages over the wall and they had to race Mumma to the package. Benne usually got to the package first and ran off with it, Mumma shouting, "Leave it! Leave it!" Benne was old enough now to "Leave it", but it was still fun to run off with things. He brought it back to Mumma, unharmed, but damp. Mumma tried to not get too frustrated with Benne.

And all throughout the week things happened they could only see if they were outside on the piazza: arguments between enforcers and offenders, city maintenance crews filling potholes, skateboarders, cyclists, people walking and jogging. It was an active neighborhood.

Saturday finally came and Dad collected his farmers' market tote bags. Benne and Scout hopped up and down, excited they were going to go to the market. Mumma reminded Dad to actually buy some vegetables and not all meat and pasta, and Dad said okay. Then he clipped their leashes on and they walked to Marion Square. Benne felt like he knew the route this time so he tried to pull them along. He was in a hurry to get there, to get lost and to ask Clementine questions.

Then they saw Clementine. There she was, out pulling a carriage in the street while the driver lectured the passengers on the history of Charleston.

"And if a gentleman saw a lady's ankle, he had to marry her on the spot!" stated the driver loudly.

"Scout!" whispered Benne. "What if Clementine isn't at the barn?"

"I guess we'll have to hide and wait!" Scout said. He hadn't thought this might happen. He wondered what else he had miscalculated.

With feelings of dread, they continued their walk with Dad.

The Farmers' Market was hot and crowded. All Scout and Benne could see were legs and feet. Lots of people stopped to pet them. Slowly they made their way around the market until the bags were full of fresh pastas and cuts of meat. Scout and Benne slowly obscured themselves under a bush while Dad talked to a friend while selecting okra from a large bin. Scout was able to get the leashes out of his hands and together they slunk off to heavier coverage so no one could see them.

Suddenly, they heard, "Look! An adorable Springer Spaniel puppy!" The ground shook as several people bounded their way. Scout looked around for an escape. He saw it! A huge sewer drain was wide open. The cover must have been stolen or removed. He had been in there before and could go into the sewer again.

"Run, Benne Wafer! Follow me!" Scout sprinted to the hole in the pavement. Benne panicked. He saw where Scout was going and knew he had to follow him. Still, it would be better to stay with Dad and be patted by all these nice people.

"Do you want some enforcer to turn YOU into a carriage mule?" barked Scout. "We have to stop this craziness or we'll all be turned into mules! Jump!"

Scout dove into the sewer hole. Benne was scared but he followed. Scout was right. It was up to them to save everyone they knew from being cursed and turned into carriage mules.

CHAPTER 7 - DOWN IN THE SEWERS OF CHARLESTON

The sewer was just as Scout remembered it – dank and dark. But it was cooler than the street surface. Summer was coming fast. Immediately, Benne Wafer landed on top of him. The little bundle smacked Scout on the back.

"Ow!" said Scout.

"I didn't see you there," said Benne. "I'm sorry. But you did make a nice cushion to fall upon."

Scout huffed. His eyes began to adjust to the dark.

"Where are we?" asked Benne.

"Under King Street. I think we can get to the Market area from here. Maybe Clementine will be back from her tour by the time we get there. Now, let's see, which way should we go?"

The puppy said he had no idea, and Scout would not have taken his advice anyway since Benne was so young a creature. Scout decided to head south. He thought it felt like he was heading toward the harbor, and being a spaniel, that seemed like a good idea.

They walked and walked. Benne's eyes bulged in his little face. He had never seen such dankness. It was much darker and chillier in the sewer than under his house where he hid the tulip bulbs weeks ago. He stuck close to Scout. They passed several intersections and Scout led them straight through.

Suddenly, they came upon an intersection and two very large wharf rats stood in their way.

"What's up, fluffy house dogs?" asked a rat that wore mirrored sunglasses.

"Nobody gets through here without paying a toll," said another rat with spikey bangs that stood up between his ears. "What've you got?" he asked. He also had on sunglasses.

Benne hid behind Scout. These rats were almost as large as Scout, and certainly larger than he.

"I don't have anything to give you," growled Scout.

"Yes, you do." Spikey pointed at the puppy. "That looks like good eatin', right there!" He grinned a horrible scary grin with big sharp teeth and took a step toward them.

"Palmetto bug?" said a voice, more as a threat than a polite offer. It came out of the darkness and the speaker was nowhere to be seen.

The rats looked around them and inhaled, "Huh?"

Chisolm waddled into the spotlight created by a perforated storm drain over his head. His front teeth were bared, gleaming.

"I said, 'Palmetto bug?', you terribly mean rats."

"Oh, Chisolm, I didn't see you in all this gloom. It is I, Morris," said the rat with the mirrored sunglasses.

"Oh, please," said Chisolm, tossing a few bugs at Spikey. "You remember Scout, don't you?"

"Well, I suppose."

Chisolm glared at Morris. "You *do* remember the tulip bulb incident not too long ago. You were 'passing through' under Scout's very own house and explained to that puppy right over there what a bulb was. You had one in your satchel!"

"It was from next door," Morris reminded Chisolm. Then he knew he was caught.

"My, what a short memory wharf rats must have," pondered Chisolm. "Well, since you recall you know these two, you won't mind a few palmetto bugs as a toll." He tossed a few more bugs at Spikey who gobbled them up immediately.

"Spike! Leave some for the rest of us!" admonished Morris.

Chisolm hurried Scout and Benne Wafer away from the squabbling rats. He knew they were turning into Market Street and would be close to the horse barn soon.

CHAPTER 8 – THE HORSE BARN

Chisolm peeked out of the gutter drain and motioned for the others to follow him as he squeezed out and darted into the dark barn. It smelled of fresh hay and farm animals. Chisolm hid behind some tall green buckets and waited for Scout to hurry Benne Wafer along on his short legs.

"Hi, there!" said a cheerful voice.

Chisolm jumped. Then he turned to see the friendly speaker.

A large Billy Goat was peering at him from between two wooden slats that made up his pen.

"Oh!" said Chisolm. "You startled me!"

Scout and Benne arrived and dove behind the buckets next to Chisolm and also came face to face with the goat.

"Hi, Zap!" said Benne, pleased to see his new friend again. "I know him!" he said to Chisolm and Scout.

"Yes, I can see our puppy has returned. Will you be staying with us this time? And your friends?" Zap chewed his hay slowly.

Scout just stared at Zap's curved horns in silence. Benne was on a first name basis with this weird-looking fellow?

"Hello, again," said a second goat, coming up next to Zap.

"And this is Zip! Zip and Zap, these are my best friends, Scout and Chisolm!" Benne hopped up and down, basking in his importance with his elders.

Scout found his voice. "He's not your puppy. He's our puppy. He lives on Montagu Street with us."

"OK, then," said Zap. "Glad you could stop in for a visit then. What brings you in today?"

Benne asked, "Is Clementine back from her tour?"

"Yes, I am," Clementine said from the rear of the barn.

Benne led the others over to her stall. Zip and Zap followed along inside their pen.

Benne stopped outside her stall. She swung her large head over the gate and sniffed him and he wiggled. Then he sneezed.

"I remember you," she said.

"We have good news, Clementine," squeaked Benne.

"Well, that'll be the day." She yawned. Then pawed the ground with her hoof. "Tell me. I'm dying of curiosity."

"Oh!" said Benne.

Scout decided to help out Benne, who was clearly intimidated by this mule, or whatever she was.

"We can maybe turn you back into a human," Scout said quietly.

Clementine's floppy ears perked forward.

"How?"

"Well," said Chisolm, joining in now. "It seems the parking enforcers have special machines that not only issue tickets and citations, but can also curse you and, in very difficult situations, turn the offender - " Clementine frowned at Chisolm " – or *perceived* offender," he amended, "into someone or something else." He folded his neat little pink paws on his furry gray tummy and grinned.

"Great," said Clementine, taking an acute interest. "Let's do it. Where's the machine? I've had all I can take hauling this wagon around. And it's not even an attractive wagon. The pretty horses get to pull the pretty white carriages. And the wedding carriages. I'm not sure if it's ironic or not that after being an almost-bridesmaid, I'm not allowed to pull a bridal carriage."

All the friends stared at Clementine.

"Wow," said Zip. "That's the most Clementine's ever talked except when she told Benne here the story last week!"

Zap nodded his horns up and down in agreement.

Benne looked at Scout and whispered, "What's *ironic* mean, Scout?"

Scout shook his head, fluffing his ears, trying to put the meaning into words for Benne, and grudgingly wishing (almost) that Pudge were here this minute. He was a walking dictionary!

"Um," said Scout. "I think it means when something the opposite of what you expect happens."

"And it might be hilarious," added Chisolm.

"Or it might not," said Clementine. "So? Do you have the magical parking enforcer's machine?"

Scout shook his head, flapping his lips and ears, and sat down. "Hmm," he said. "We seemed to have overlooked that detail. Where can we get one, Chisolm?"

Chisolm said, "That's easy. We'll follow an enforcer and when he or she puts it down, we'll grab it."

"And then what?" asked Clementine. "Do you know how to use it? What if you turn me into something worse?"

A fly buzzed around her ears and she moved them back and forth, trying to discourage the fly.

"Well, we've never actually looked at one up close," said Benne, "but they seemed to have a lot of buttons. Maybe it's clearly marked, which one we should push."

Scout and Chisolm brightened at this suggestion.

"OK," said Chisolm. "I'll handle this. There are bunches of enforcers walking around this area. I'll just follow one until maybe they put down the machine to eat lunch."

"And what if that poor enforcer gets into trouble for losing their ticket machine?" asked Zap.

"Hmm," said Scout again. Then he said, "Maybe we'll only need it for a few minutes and then we can take it back, or leave it where it can be found by an enforcer."

"This doesn't sound like much of a plan to me," said Clementine, "but give a shot, please!"

"Great," said Chisolm. "We'll leave Benne Wafer here since he's very small."

Benne pouted. Zap licked Benne on the head to reassure him.

"Scout, let's go."

The possum and the spaniel quickly left the barn while Benne scooted into the goats' pen to hide from any carriage workers. He had to see Clementine turned back into a person!

CHAPTER 9 – THE TICKET MACHINE

Scout really felt bad about stealing, but Chisolm assured him over and over they were simply borrowing. Still, Scout had his doubts as he followed Chisolm to the busier part of the market area.

The enforcers were not hard to spot. They wore navy blue pants and shirts and a yellow vest. Today a pair was checking for expired meters.

Scout and Chisolm hid behind a city garbage can next to a low wall. They could hear the enforcers chatting about every day things and rude people, when it happened!

Chisolm just loved it when he could predict how things would play out and then they did!

The enforcer laid her ticket machine on the top of the wall and went off with the other enforcer. They said something about lunch.

"Psst! Scout! Now's our chance. Grab it and run!"

Scout wasted no time. The instant he grabbed it with his mouth, the enforcers turned and saw him.

"Stop!" they yelled.

Scout ran as fast as he could away from them, but not straight to the barn. He wanted to give them the slip so he

could return to the barn with enough time to spare so that
he could examine the machine and then use it to un-curse
poor Clementine.

Meanwhile, Chisolm slipped into a nearby drain to
head back to the barn and to wait for Scout!

Scout held the clunky heavy thing in his jaws and raced
down North Market Street toward State Street, the
shoulder strap flying behind him. As he rounded the
corner and dashed through the basket-weaving ladies, he
saw a large van barreling down State Street right at him.
Now he veered left, up some steps and found himself
inside a restaurant. Some tourists that were waiting for
tables gasped and one lady said, "There's a dog in here!"

Scout knew he had made a mistake. Luckily, he could
see an exit on the other side of the restaurant and he raced
towards it. The shoulder strapped snagged on a chair leg
briefly, but he gave it a good yank and the chair went flying
across the room, straight into a waitress who was carrying
a huge tray of raw oysters. He didn't have time to watch
the chaos, but he heard the shells raining down on the
hardwood floor and people shouting.

Back into the sunlight he blinked. Which way was the barn? He sniffed and his sharp sense of smell led him from the restaurant, through the covered market stalls and to the horse barn. He darted through a side door. The wagons on the street were loaded with tourists and hot teams of horses stood patiently, swatting flies with their tails.

"Whew!" said Scout when he arrived at the goats' pen. He dropped the ticket machine and stared at it. He knew they didn't have much time.

The ticket machine was the most indecipherable object Scout had ever seen. It had a little screen, which was blank, and about nine buttons with strange markings on them.

Benne Wafer popped out of small pile of hay. "Wow! Cool! You got it, Scout!" He hopped up and down.

"Shh!" cautioned Chisolm, who reappeared next to Benne.

Zip and Zap stood close to Benne. Zip asked, "Now what do we do with it?"

"Hmm," said Scout.

The group was silent, staring at the gray object. Beyond them, Clementine snorted.

"OK, what's going on? Did you get it?" She stretched her neck as far as she could to see the group.

"Yes, Scout got it! He got it!" squeaked Benne.

Chisolm whispered to Scout, "Which button do we press?"

"How should I know?" Scout whispered back.

Benne, impatient with his elders, snatched the shoulder strap and raced to Clementine's stall. He nudged the front end, what he believed was the front end, to point at Clementine's hoof and pressed a button with his nose.

"Benne!" shouted Scout. "Stop!"

"Stop! Stop!" shouted the goats and the possum.

But Benne had made his choice. The big purple button on the first row look like a good guess according to his puppy logic.

A faint burning smell wafted up from the straw beneath Clementine's feet. Benne raced back to the others.

Sparks flew and smoked clouded the barn. One of the barn workers shouted, "Fire!" and they could hear the sirens from the fire station on Meeting Street approaching the barn rapidly.

The possum and the dogs ran from the barn to hidden safety beneath the porch of a restaurant in an alley and watched while the workers quickly evacuated the goats and other horses. The fire engines arrived and their hoses rained water on the barn. Still, the barn workers hadn't noticed Clementine missing…

A loud screeching sound filled the air. The roof collapsed.

Someone now shouted Clementine's name, and another argued she was out on a tour, and the other shouted back she turned up lame after her tour so she had the rest of the day off from tours. The crowd that gathered by now was horrified. The barn workers were horrified. Poor Clementine… if she was still inside…

A roar louder than the siege of Charleston now silenced the crowd. And a high, echoing screech, and another.

A gigantic purple and green dragon reared its head from inside the barn and looked around at the market area, crowd and firemen.

She seemed to smack her lips and make a big decision. She drew up her green and purple scaly wings over her and flapped them a few times, like an experiment. The wind nearly flattened the crowd.

Then she took flight, rising up into the air, circling the Market. As if experimenting again, she opened her mouth and exhaled.

Shiny hot fire burst forth and touched off the barn again. The firemen scrambled to turn the hoses on the new flames.

Meanwhile, the rescue group hid under the porch and their little mouths hung open as they stared at Clementine still circling, trying to gather her bearings and wits. They cringed as she almost clipped St. Michael's church on a flyby.

"See?" said Scout to Benne who tried to melt into the ground by becoming very flat. "See what happens when you don't listen? When you go off and do whatever and you have no idea what you're doing?"

"Yes," agreed Chisolm sternly, frowning at Benne.

"Yes, it's very clear what happens," said Zap.

"Yes," agreed Zip. "You get a purple fire-breathing dragon that has no idea how to fly instead of a cynical mule."

CHAPTER 10 - CLEMENTINE THE DRAGON

"Goodness," said Chisolm that night in Scout's backyard during their last let-out before bedtime.

"What a day." Scout shook his head. Benne sat a little distance away from the pair. He was still in a bit of trouble with everyone.

Mumma and Dad had collected them from the restaurant. One of the nice staff recognized their phone number on Scout's collar and called them immediately. They watched the firemen clear out of the area and wondered about the dragon.

"Does insurance cover damage by dragons?" wondered a diner near by.

"I positively doubt it," said Mumma.

Chisolm had scuttled home through the sewers. And Zip and Zap were taken to another barn.

"I wonder what will happen to Clementine?" wondered Benne out loud.

Scout scowled and just then they saw a flame flicker in the corner of the garden.

"Psst," said the dragon.

They jumped. Clementine's eyes glowed in the darkness.

"Please don't burn our house down," said Scout. "We like living here.

"Hey, I'm trying to get the hang of this as fast as I can," growled Clementine. "Have you ever tried to fly?"

"No," admitted Chisolm. "Is it fun?"

"More fun than you could ever guess. That's why I stopped by."

They waited.

"To thank Benne Wafer. He picked the right button. I love being a dragon. At least I think I do."

"But where will you live?" asked Scout. "I don't think people here will get used to you flying around here."

"Oh, well, I've been thinking about it. I'm not sure. Maybe the Galapagos Islands. I might fit in better there with those big lizards. I visited there once when I was in college."

"Is that a long way from Charleston?" asked Benne Wafer.

Clementine grinned. "Yes, Benne Wafer, the
Galapagos Islands are indeed a long way from
Charleston."

"Will you come back and visit us?" asked Benne.

Clementine smiled and snorted a little smoke, leaning
her great scaly head next to Benne's little soft furry body.

"Absolutely. Especially if I decide I want to be turned
into something else. But not a carriage mule!"

Benne wiggled and Scout and Chisolm patted
Clementine's scaly green head.

The back door light came on. Clementine stretched
her wings and – *whoosh!* – rose straight up in the air and
flew off into the night for more Southern skies.

The three friends could not see Clementine flying away
in the night sky. She was invisible to anyone searching for
a dragon.

"Goodness," said Chisolm again. "What an exciting
day!" He burrowed into his rosemary bush for a quick nap
before some midnight foraging. Scout and Benne,
yawning, agreed with Chisolm. Friends again, they went
inside and up to their comfortable round dog beds for a
long nap. If they had made friends with a dragon today,

who knew what tomorrow would bring? Certainly new friends and new adventures for a pair of black and white Springer Spaniels and a possum called Chisolm.

The End

ABOUT THE AUTHOR

Nancy Lucas lives in Charleston, South Carolina with her husband and a silly Springer Spaniel who won't let her get any work done because he wants to play *all* day.

http://nancylucas.com/blog

Made in the USA
Monee, IL
18 December 2020